What people are saying about

# The War for Islam

*The War for Islam* projects the struggle between the two sides
of Islam, extremist and moderate, onto a troubled and violent
world a hundred years in the future. Its heroes are two Muslim
women and a Christian man struggling to free the world from
a counterfeit religion intent on world domination. Written by a
professor of world religions, the novel spans the globe, from
Japan to Sudan, from Belgium to India, and works brilliantly at
both the geopolitical and personal levels. Betty has undertaken a
uniquely ambitious project. His novel raises profoundly important
questions and delights the reader along the way.
**Norman Prigge, Ph.D.** Associate Professor of Philosophy, retired

# The War
# for Islam

# The War
# for Islam

Stafford Betty

Winchester, UK
Washington, USA

First published by Roundfire Books, 2019
Roundfire Books is an imprint of John Hunt Publishing Ltd., No. 3 East St., Alresford,
Hampshire SO24 9EE, UK
office1@jhpbooks.net
www.johnhuntpublishing.com
www.roundfire-books.com

For distributor details and how to order please visit the 'Ordering' section on our website.

Text copyright: Stafford Betty 2018

ISBN: 978 1 78904 042 5
978 1 78904 043 2 (ebook)
Library of Congress Control Number: 2018932802

A CIP catalogue record for this book is available from the British Library.

Design: Stuart Davies

UK: Printed and bound by CPI Group (UK) Ltd, Croydon, CR0 4YY
US: Printed and bound by Thomson Shore, 7300 West Joy Road, Dexter, MI 48130

Also by this Author...

Fiction

Ghost Boy

978-1-78535-798-5 Paperback

978-1-78535-799-2 E-book


Non-Fiction

The Afterlife Unveiled

978-1-84694-496-3 Paperback

978-1-84694-926-5 E-book

We operate a distinctive and ethical publishing philosophy in
all areas of our business, from our global network of authors to
production and worldwide distribution.

# Chapter 1

Saira Marwat, dressed in a swallowing gray niqab with only her hands and eyes showing, pushed a baby carriage full of groceries home. It was a cool October evening, and the next call to prayer was fifteen minutes away. Brooklyn was at its best with all the yellow-orange leaves rustling in the plane trees, lindens, and maples overhead. The minaret on the other side of the street was all the accent needed for a perfect late afternoon walk — if only it had led to a different destination.

Saira lived in an upscale house on Tilden Avenue in East Flatbush with her forty-three-year-old husband, Rasool; his senior wife, Afeefa; and Afeefa's two children, a son and a daughter. Before her marriage she lived in fear of her father and endured the repressive conditions imposed on her as best she could — she had what her father called an "attitude." By the time she reached high school she was already asking questions that alarmed both her parents and her teachers at the madrasa, where she far excelled all of the other students, both in brains and beauty. Why did Muslim girls wear the veil while Christians did not? Why did married non-Muslim women get to work jobs while married Muslim women had to stay home? Why did Christian males restrict themselves to one wife, while Muslims could have as many as four? Was it really true that Christians thought the prophet Jesus was God? That seemed too preposterous to be true. And why did Christians condemn all honor killing? Did they just walk away when their loved ones were murdered? Without going so far as to doubt her faith, she couldn't help feeling curious about the world that might exist outside it.

But her father ruled her with an iron fist and locked out the answers available on her smartphone and computer. He even talked to the fathers of her friends and warned them about

1

a possible influence. Rasool imposed the same smothering conditions on her once they married. She had a job as a secretary at Asmaul Husna College, once St. Joseph's College, but bought long ago by a Saudi conglomerate. She loved her job, but liked it better before her marriage when she could wear a dress that revealed her figure or, on a rare day when she "went American," even jeans. Now she had to wear the niqab. Every evening Rasool interrogated her on what she might have heard at work. All employees at the university were supposed to be Muslim, but there were too many Muslims with dangerous ideas to suit him. "Why can't you get pregnant?" he asked her over and over. Then she wouldn't have an excuse to work outside the home, and he wouldn't have to worry. She wanted a child, but not yet. So she took birth control pills on the sly, leaving Rasool without a clue. As for the niqab, she found it a walking prison. Unlike many Muslim women, who proudly wore it by choice, she wore it because Rasool made her. At least he allowed her eye slits: After a screaming fit he permitted her to remove the mesh covering her lovely dark eyes.

"You walked all the way home?" Afeefa greeted her in the usual exhausted voice, as if the world should pity her. "Rasool won't be home until seven." That meant a break in Afeefa's routine.

Afeefa was the cook and housekeeper. Saira, at nineteen, was the doll. But the doll had dodged pregnancy. What was left of Afeefa's self-respect was still intact.

Saira threw off the niqab, then reached into her drawer of sexy bras and panties. Yes, that was his favorite, she thought, as she lifted out a sequined red bikini bottom with a bra to match; and the short skirt would go nice on top. They had little to share by way of conversation, but she knew how to press his buttons. "You actually like your wife?" she once overheard him exclaim to a stranger at a party. "I have two wives, but I don't like either one of them!" She couldn't forget that insult, and she found it hard to forgive, even though she liked him no better. It made her try all the harder to enslave him with her wiles. She did a good job of it.

The call to prayer, the *naghrib*, sounded from the mosque, and she fell to her knees after covering herself with a sheet and touched the floor with her forehead.

# Chapter 2

Silas Wyatt was a lean, bearded man of above-average height with an intensely serious air about him. Christian by birth, he somehow managed to stay Christian, actually more or less Roman Catholic, while watching his friends slip away. It wasn't so much an ardor for the faith that kept him going, but the absence of anything better and a deep-seated belief that religion of some kind was essential for human happiness. So at the age of twenty-five he found himself in a Ph.D. program at the University of Chicago's Divinity School. His specialty was the History of Christianity, with secondary emphases on Islamic Studies and Hinduism. Rigor was the order of the day: Greek, Latin, and Arabic shared equal space with his historical studies. It was a hell of a load.

Si, as his few friends called him, was more than a scholar in training. When he was twenty-two, with a whole summer free to do as he liked before he hauled off to Chicago from his home in Madison, Wisconsin, he studied, partly for fun, the claims of psychical researchers about the afterlife, especially readings that claimed to be channeled from spirits. He wasn't sure they were what they seemed, but something they claimed—universally, as far as he could tell—was that everybody existed prior to birth and came to earth with a plan, a hoped-for destiny, but that few ever succeeded in achieving it. Something about this made total sense to him, and he was sure he hadn't planned on being a scholar. But what *had* he planned? He didn't know, but words like *herald, shepherd, provider,* and once or twice *man of destiny* kept turning up in his imagination. So he went to graduate school to study religion, learn how to provide, and see what he was destined to do, if anything. In any case, he fully intended to be among those rare souls who succeeded.

Almost daily he doubted the value of all the preparation

forced on him by the program. What did ancient Greek and Latin have to do with the events of the day? Now Arabic he could understand. Islam was the pivot point on which world history was turning in the year 2090. France was 45 percent Muslim and Belgium 95 percent, with sharia firmly established there. Television revealed a whole population tightly tucked in between France, Germany, and the Netherlands that had little resemblance to its neighbors: No woman, including non-Muslims, would dare show her skin in public. The burqa ruled. As for London, terrorists were bombing night clubs, restaurants, and theaters on a nearly weekly basis. And in India, with its prodigious population of 2.1 billion, suicide attacks on temples were so frequent that they didn't even make the news. Hinduism was faltering; its love for its gods was losing ground to the Caliphate's hatred of them. East Asia was another battleground. Mindanao, the southernmost major island of the Philippines, was squarely in the hands of the United Caliphate, with all churches destroyed and black banners waving over every major building. The region's Catholic population had either converted, fled, or been put to death. Only Japan and Australia had successfully resisted the radical face of the Caliphate. Silas looked upon all this with alarm.

As for America, its population of 470 million was roughly divided into five sectors: 30 percent Christian, 19 percent Muslim, 31 percent "nones," 9 percent atheist/secular, and 11 percent everything else, including Jews, Hindus, Buddhists, Sikhs, and Spiritualists. Fifty percent of Michigan was Muslim, and 45 percent of Maine. Terrorism was on the rise. The latest bombing was of California's high-speed rail that sent a train traveling at 190 mph hurtling into a ravine, killing nearly everyone on board. The havoc looked more like a plane crash, and the Caliphate was happy to claim responsibility. Many Americans called for revenge, and for a few weeks Muslims hunkered down in their neighborhoods. Politicians universally spoke out against retaliation but disagreed profoundly over what to do about it. American Muslims overwhelmingly condemned the goal of the Caliphate—85 percent according to the latest Pew poll—which was to take over the world for Allah. In Si's classes Muslims spoke out fearlessly against their radicalized brothers, whom they called "the predators." Yet all these good Muslims never took to the streets to condemn the latest violence and seldom expressed themselves in print.

One of Silas's classmates, Layla Haddad, made his heart stir when he came across her on campus. He had never met a woman he felt more drawn to, more comfortable with. She wore the hijab—on this particular day a beautiful green veil with orange trim that tightly gripped her face, hiding her ears. There was nothing about that face to qualify for *Vogue*, nothing dazzling or sexy. But in her expression was the inner beauty of a quiet soul at peace with herself and her world. Si found himself deeply attracted. When he thought of marriage, a rather far-off, purely theoretical musing, it was only with her. She knew nothing of his feelings, or if she did, she kept it to herself.

On this particular April day sitting with her in the cafeteria after a class on Christian-Muslim Dialog, he felt the warm glow of her presence settle over him. How was he so lucky to be Layla's friend? Why was she not sitting with some other classmate, better looking and more affable?

# Chapter 3

Tariq al-Brooklyni—that was his adopted name—stood in front of the usual black flag tacked to the wall behind him in the spacious Bronx apartment that doubled as home for his family and recruiting center. He brandished an ancient Kalashnikov rifle in one hand and adjusted a bandolier worn over his shoulder with the other.

"Let me see your finger, brothers!" Instantly thirteen index fingers shot up.

"What does that stand for, brothers?"

"Victory over the oppressors!" shouted one of the young men, most still in their late teens, all sitting on the floor in the sparsely furnished room.

"What are you? Heretics? Is that the first thing that comes to mind?"

Quiet.

"It stands for the oneness of Allah, brothers. No partners, no God-man, do you hear? Just God. And what else? You can put your hands down now."

Again, quiet. Tariq's intensity was intimidating. His wavy brown curls and light eyes belonged to a man his parents had christened Vladimir but whose change of faith was not matched by a change in appearance. His was the new look. "Fit in, give no clues to the oppressors," his own recruiter commanded him three years ago. He looked like a California surfer, but his intensity, that was something else.

"It means the rejection of any other way. It means the Quran only. It means universal sharia. It means the end of compromise with the West. It means death to the pluralism and corruption all around us, even in Islam—especially in Islam. It means jihad. Look over to your right. What do you see against the wall?"

Quiet, then one of the recruits said, "Our suicide vests?"

"No, brothers! It's your martyr's vest! *Suicide* is a word the enemy has invented to confuse you. Those are your entry tickets into Paradise. Tonight. Tonight in Central Park, just as we've planned. The New York Philharmonic will be giving their usual July 4 concert. They'll be making that decadent noise they call music. Do you hear me? You are the bravest of our recruits, true *shaheeds*. You volunteered all you have to give. But death is not to be feared. Death is the desired goal for a martyr, not a necessary evil. Always bear in mind the motto of the martyr: 'I fight, therefore I exist.' Your reward will be the greatest imaginable... Any questions?"

Tariq waited for a mere two seconds, then called out to his wife, "Hapipah."

Dressed in a stylish tan burqa decorated with arabesque patterns in blue and gold, Hapipah brought in homemade cookies on a lacquered black tray. She looked at her husband and said in an accent, "Dishes are in the kitchen. And bowls for ice cream, vanilla and chocolate. And glasses for iced tea. I used our wedding set. I hope you don't mind."

He nodded with unsmiling dignity, then said, "What they are destined for is better than a thousand weddings."

After refreshments the recruits settled back in their places to listen to Tariq's final message. They knew he was just getting started. They had heard only the warmup.

Muhammad Caspary was one of those recruits. His home was Sunset Park, a Muslim neighborhood in Brooklyn, but he never felt at home, even there. He didn't get along with people, especially his older brother, who slapped him around when he brought home bad grades in school. No one invited him to join in a game or just hang around, and he lacked the confidence to put himself forward. So he made the Internet his world, and it was there he discovered the beauty of the Caliphate and its grand purpose—and his particular destiny.

At 8:30 p.m., with the concert already under way, he

disembarked from the maxicab Tariq hired. Six of his "*shaheed* buddies" had already alighted, and six would follow—all thirteen of them, every 200 yards or so, along Fifth Avenue between 79th and 85th Streets. In this way, Tariq thought, suspicion would be averted.

It was a beautiful evening, cool for July after the rain, so the jackets they wore over their vests did not look out of place. The plan was to blow themselves up near the end of Tchaikovsky's *1812 Overture,* all together at the same time when the fireworks began. The crowd was projected to be around 350,000, and each recruit, at some distance from every other, was responsible for his own sector. It would be an extravagant display of well-coordinated force designed to terrorize the world out of its godless slumber.

Muhammad walked west toward the music and the immense throng spread out over lush grass that served as the floor of the park's Great Lawn. It was music he did not understand, and the people littering the grass with their quilts and sipping their wine he disliked intensely, even the Muslim women wearing their hijabs. Why had he not expected to see Muslims in the crowd? There were even a few in burqas.

Unnerved but determined, he artfully stepped around people toward his sector on the west side. He suddenly felt a horror at what he was about to do. To settle himself he called to mind what Tariq had said the day before. *Remember…there are only two camps: Dar al-Islam, the House of Islam, and Dar al-Harb, the House of War, the House of Heresy…and it's up to you, each of you, to restore the House of Islam…if you do not fight to restore it, you will inherit hell.*

But why the killing of civilians? His mother once told him that if he ever killed anybody she would send him to hell herself. At the time he was sure she was just a woman who did not understand. Now he wasn't so sure. Now he understood why Tariq made them memorize Quran 2:216: *Fighting is ordered for you even though you dislike it and it may be that you dislike a thing that is good for you and like a thing that is bad for you. Allah knows but you do not know.* Muhammad realized that he disliked a thing that was good for him, that was all, and he breathed a little easier.

But still he dreaded the thought of killing Muslims, even if they were wishy-washy. He began to inspect his sector, but it was getting dark, and it wasn't easy to see where the least damage could be done. He found himself shivering, fearing the thing that was "good for him to do."

He remembered verse 4:29, the prohibition in the Quran against taking one's own life: *And do not kill yourselves. Surely, Allah is Most Merciful to you.* At one time he thought the meaning was crystal clear. But Tariq, again, came to his aid. *Yes, innocents are often victims in a Holy War. But they are martyrs too. And as for you, it's suicide if you take your life out of depression and despair, but martyrdom if for the victory of Islam. Do not fear! Fear instead your fear! The purest joy in Islam is to kill and be killed for Allah."*

The *1812 Overture* began, and Muhammad, to his surprise, began to fear the loss of his own life. He thought he was beyond such petty selfishness, but as he looked down at his feet standing on the green grass of Central Park, he felt a kind of nostalgia for the world he would be leaving behind. Appalled, he called to mind the various rewards for the martyr. *Why do you cling to this world when the next world is better?* This was the clear message of the Quran and all the hadith. Paradise was real and full of delights. He could expect beautiful gardens, palm trees, gushing springs, low-hanging fruit, delicious meat, wine that didn't intoxicate, peaceful homes with fine carpets, handsome couches and beds, dignified speech, and a harem of virgins. But for some reason these delights seemed strangely irrelevant as the music played on and the moment of death approached. He found himself beginning to shiver violently.

The moment came. The first fireworks boomed into the sky, sending a shower of streaming light heavenward. Muhammad stood up and scanned the crowd, both ahead and behind. Flashes he saw and booms he heard. His brothers had not flinched. The people close around him, the victims he had chosen, stood up and wondered what was happening. Were they to be *surrounded* by fireworks? At first they marveled, but then they heard what sounded like a woman's scream, a distant scream. Still they did not grasp what was happening. "Look, darling," said a mother to her little son just ten feet from where Muhammad stood. "Isn't it beautiful? Don't you wish Daddy was here!"

Now there were screams closer by, and the crowd became restless and began to break up. "The orchestra stopped playing!" said someone. "Something's wrong!" Muhammad removed the safety and placed his finger on the trigger. It was now or never. He thought of his mother's warning. He thought of the little boy whose mother was scooping him up to run for safety. Would he destroy them? Never before in his life had there been so perfect a balance of the scale between doing and not doing. But the balance had to tip. It wasn't fear of dying that tipped it. It was fear of killing. He took his finger off the trigger and, absurdly, joined the crowd in its flight. But to where? He saw the dark shapes of trees to the south and ran in that direction away from the crowd that scattered east and west—yes, ran, but from whom, from what? He slowed to a walk and remembered something else Tariq said: *It's easier to die for something you believe in than to kill for it.* He hadn't understood at the time, but now he did. Dying he could do, but killing was beyond him.

He reached a cluster of trees as helicopters flew overhead with their lights shining on the mayhem below while sirens blared. But around him, hidden by trees and bushes, there was only stillness. Nothing moved, no one to kill. He pressed the trigger and blew himself up into a thousand pieces.

# Chapter 4

Silas's heart sank when he heard the news of the slaughter at Central Park. He was in his room in Madison working on his dissertation when the news hit. "Son, you've got to hear this," came the call from his dad who was watching TV.

His first thought was to call Layla, but he wasn't completely sure how she would take it. After all, Islam was her religion, even though she abhorred what was sometimes done in its name, and it was already past nine. But he didn't have to think about it for long because she called him from her home in Libertyville, just north of Chicago.

"Si, did you hear?"

"Layla, oh, this is too horrible. I was about to call. Then you called first. It's appalling."

"Oh my God, this world must be making God weep! We need a race of superior aliens to swoop down on us and bring order! It makes your thesis all the more urgent because the only help we're going to get will come from us."

"Right. You know, I'm thinking of traveling to New York and interviewing the families of victims, the families of bombers, Muslims of all stripes, Christians too, fundies and liberals, anybody and everybody. I'm thinking of restricting my dissertation to an analysis of this particular event rather than to Islamist terror in general."

"New York. My God, Si. But what's needed is the big picture. You have so much to say about that. Don't limit yourself."

"Wouldn't it be wonderful if Muslims were to organize and march by the thousands into the Park. Maybe bring gifts to the very spot of the carnage. You know, be proactive at last. Take to the streets. Dammit, take to the streets! Call the radical bastards out! This is a Muslim problem, and it's going to take Muslims to solve it."

"You're right, Si. It is a Muslim problem. And you know what? If there *was* such a march, I'd fly there to be a part of it. Too bad it'll never happen."

"Yeah, too bad." There was a pause in the conversation as if to allow sadness to have its say. Then Silas blurted out, "For Christ's sake, Layla, why don't *you* organize it?"

"Yeah, sure."

"I'm serious. Maybe all it takes is a phone call to the mayor's office to get it started. Just a little guts. What's there to lose? Just call the mayor or somebody and offer to organize a march. What the hell? Why not? I'll help you."

"You're a funny man, Silas. Seriously, what are you talking about?"

"We're in summer break, Layla. We're unemployed. What do we have to do besides read all day long?"

"Then you do it."

"Not a chance. It's got to come from a Muslim. And you're it. But I'll be right behind you. Your shadow."

"Can you really imagine me doing such a thing?"

"Look, I've just looked up the mayor's office. All you have to do is call it. See what happens. Here's the number." He read out the number and told her to take it down.

"This is ridiculous. But for you I'll do it, do it tomorrow morning."

"Let me know how it goes. But remember: make it clear you're a Muslim, and that you want to lead a march, a *Muslim* march, against the Caliphate. And that you're a graduate student at the University of Chicago. That'll give you credibility."

"Okay. I'll do it."

Silas and Layla were amazed by their New York reception after what had begun back in Madison as little more than a crazy idea, just a dare that led to a phone call. After landing at Newark Airport, they were whisked away into a flying car, or "flyover," that status vehicle of the super-rich, and put up at the Marriott Essex House on the Park's southern border. From there they worked out the details of the march with the city's Community Events Director, the Parks and Recreation Commissioner, and the Police Department. The work was exhausting but exhilarating.

The *New York Times* headlined the rally as a potential sea change in intra-Islamic politics. Halfway into the article the unlikely story of how it all came together appeared:

Mayor Philip Lehrer described how two graduate students from the University of Chicago's Divinity School, first one, then the other, called his office Monday and proposed a march to the site of the massacre. He said, "They asked for a permit for Saturday and said they would fly in the next day and organize it. What sold me was their insistence that it was to be a *Muslim* protest. I greased the wheels and cut through the red tape."

One of the students, Layla Haddad, is a 24-year-old Muslim woman of Egyptian origin. When interviewed she gave credit for the event to her friend, Silas Wyatt, a 26-year-old Christian from Madison, Wisconsin, who is majoring in the history of Christianity while studying Islam and Arabic on the side. "He talked me into it, even though I thought he was being totally unrealistic. But now I am tremendously excited. We hope all Muslims who condemn this latest atrocity of the so-called Caliphate will show up. They should bring placards. They can't kill us all."

The march will move down Fifth Avenue to 85th Street and turn right onto the Great Lawn, scene of the Massacre. Mr. Wyatt, Ms. Haddad, and many of the city's imams will place wreaths on each of the twelve bombing sites. The Met tenor Ashkan Kazemi will chant Allah's ninety-nine names as the wreaths are placed. Ms. Haddad will address the crowd at the conclusion.

It could not be confirmed at press time, but Governor Dawson is rumored to attend. As for the mayor, "I wouldn't miss it! Later in the day the Yankees will play the Red Sox before 50,000 fans. What's more important?"

Layla and Si had never spent so much time together, and each admired the other's dedication and intelligence. At one point as they were finishing their lunch in the hotel restaurant, Si looked at her sitting opposite and broke out into a tired but utterly contented smile as he gulped down a glass of the house beer. Layla had never seen him so unreserved and relaxed, not even in Chicago, where his seriousness left little outlet for lightheartedness.

"This is going to be amazing, it's all come together so well," he said leaning back on his chair with one arm draped carelessly over the back, the Arabic-English dictionary on the next chair forgotten.

"You look happy," she said, as the tiny emerald stud on her nose glistened.

"I am. But you should be happier. It's your religion. You'll make the address. You'll make history. I'm your sidekick."

"No, you're not!" She laughed. "You know that's not true!"

Suddenly he leaned forward and eyed her in that incredibly serious way that both unnerved and attracted her to him and said, "Do you know, I caught a glimpse of you without your hijab as I waited for you to get ready. You know what? I think you *let* me see you that way. You did, didn't you?" He was grinning, just daring her to admit it.

"Well aren't you—aren't you—the cheeky one?" She was blushing slightly.

"I liked what I saw, Layla. Your hair is beautiful, you know. So is your handwriting. I think you must have been a Chinese calligrapher in your previous life. What do you say to that?"

She was not one for the quick comeback. Amused at the

thought, she smiled and said nothing. But Silas was not finished with his teasing. "Don't you sometimes wish you were a Christian?" he said.

"Now you've gone too far. Besides, if I were, how could I give the address tomorrow, you silly man?"

He took the last sip of his beer. "Ah, good stuff! Do you want a taste?"

"Don't be double silly. Besides, you just finished it!"

"Ah, yes, so I did." The combination of Si's rapid metabolism and that single glass of beer was just enough to make him frisky. He was having fun and in a mood to continue teasing. He could tell she was enjoying it. So he dared to say, "Layla, you're twenty-four, and with no prospect in sight. For a Muslim girl aren't you a little long in the tooth? I mean, where are you going to find a husband?"

"Oh, he'll find me—someday. I'm not worried." She was not amused.

Si was embarrassed. He had gone too far. And if he said anymore, he could damage their friendship. What he really wanted to say is that her future husband was sitting across the table from her if only she'd have him. He sighed loudly, then said, "What if the guy who found you was a Christian?"

"Well, he'd have to convert. I'm not *that* progressive."

"Yeah. Yeah, I know."

His fingers on both hands played with the glass, turning it counterclockwise, then clockwise. He seemed lost in thought as he stared at it. Without looking up he said, "Well, I guess we better go upstairs and get to work on the finishing touches."

"Okay. I'll come find you after I've rested. Don't forget your book."

# Chapter 5

In a house on Tilden Avenue in East Flatbush on the morning of the march, a young Muslim woman dressed herself in front of the bathroom mirror. She had chosen a single-tone brown dress reaching down to the top of her feet and a simple black hijab in keeping with the somber moment. She had eaten earlier and waited for the moment she could slink out of the house, without the niqab, unseen by either her husband or his senior wife. The problem was how to smuggle out the banner she had labored over the night before and hidden under her bed. She could hear her husband shaving and darted into the bedroom to grab the banner. She almost made it out the door unseen, but one of the kids saw her. She looked back to see the child with mouth open. *Allah, the Merciful, protect me!* she prayed to herself as she hurried to the subway entrance, dreading the deep male voice of her husband she imagined running after her.

It wasn't 50,000, but it was at least half that many. People of every description, not just Muslims, but Christians and Sikhs and even LGBT—you could tell by the rainbow—assembled on a warm Saturday morning where Fifth Avenue meets Central Park North, two and a half miles above the site of the massacre. Placards and banners by the hundreds left no doubt where the hearts of the marchers lay.

As the wave of humanity moved southward, they were met by cheers, but also jeers. A few of the jeers came from supporters of the Caliphate, but others came from people who were so incensed by "the Muslims" that they couldn't distinguish the good from the bad. Even when they saw placards that read, "Down with the Caliphate," or "Allah condemns suicide," or "Muslims love Christians," or "God doesn't play favorites," they didn't understand. They had come to express their hatred of Muslims, and they would not be denied.

But most of the bystanders did understand, and many joined the march as it went by when they read the signs. "These people are our friends!" they said, almost in disbelief. So they swelled the crowd.

A small refrigerator truck carried the wreaths, and imams from all over the boroughs laid them at the spots of the carnage while Kazemi intoned the 99 Names of God.

Finally, the governor and the mayor introduced Layla. The *Times* and a television interview had created a great deal of interest in her, and the crowd was eager to hear what she would say. Her speech lasted twelve minutes, only half the time it would take to read a scholarly paper at a meeting of the American Academy of Religion. But unlike those presentations, whose meaning seldom went beyond securing a promotion for the reader, this speech, as Silas predicted, would make American history.

Her speech, crafted by Layla and him working side by side in his hotel room, and never quite finished to their satisfaction, rang out. Halfway through, she launched the words that would make history:

The greatness of Islam is not in question. There is so much about it to love, to cherish. It reminds us to keep our eyes turned toward heaven, toward Allah. As our beloved Quran says, "What is the life of this world but amusement and play? But life in the Hereafter—that is truly life indeed."

But you would never guess that from what happened here a week ago. The bombers are not true Muslims. In their distrust of God to carry out his will in his own way, they defile the Muslim religion. The whole idea of a Muslim state, a so-called Caliphate, is a fiasco, a delusion. It would mean disaster for all Americans, whose country explicitly separates church from state, but for every other country in the world as well. My heart cries out for all the Coptic Christians murdered in Egypt, my grandfather's country of origin, and for those Copts who survived and finally fled the slaughter and immigrated, many to this country. That so many Muslims support this barbarism is cause for deep shame in me, and should be in you. That so many Muslims in countries all over the world call their non-Muslim sisters and brothers heretics and infidels and require them to follow their sharia, while ignoring their own sacred teachings, is cause for deep shame in me, and should be in you. That so many Muslims deny their girls access to books and pens, for fear that an educated woman is a threat to society, is cause for deep shame in me, and should be in you. That so many Muslim women are barricaded by their fathers and husbands in burqas, as if the very shape of their bodies was obscene and loathsome, is cause for deep shame in me, and should be in you. That American Muslims cry out for the right to amplify their voices as they call the faithful to prayer five times a day, yet destroy Christian churches in the lands where they form the majority, is cause for deep shame in me, and should be in you. That contemporary jihad like the massacre that occurred on this very spot a week ago is glorified by young men dressed in black waving their rifles in celebration is cause for deep shame in me, and should be in you. Let us never call this so-called religion of the Caliphate Islam.

Layla had much more to say. A call to "identify and report the murderous element in our own neighborhoods and even families" drew loud applause. So did the usual reminder that the Caliphate would never be defeated by "bombs and lasers and drones," but by "good citizen Muslims like us." "Our voices must be heard, both in the media and on the pavement, and they will be," she vowed.

When she had finished and the ceremony was closed by the

governor, she was rushed by reporters and photographers who couldn't get enough of her. A few marchers hung around, one a young woman with a furled banner in her hand and black hijab covering her head. She stood patiently in a brown dress under the unclouded sun as she studied Layla and tried to catch every word. No one noticed her until the last reporter put away his recorder and Layla's shoulders slumped in exhaustion.

The woman in the brown dress rushed up to Layla and knelt on one knee before her with hands folded in front of her face. "Oh, thank you, thank you, thank you!" she said. "Do you have time to talk to me? Just for a few minutes?" The lines on her face told of an earnestness that touched the heart.

At that moment a policeman motioned Layla over to him. "Just a minute," Layla said to the strange young woman. She then turned to the policeman.

"We need to get you back to your hotel," he said. "We've received death threats."

Layla lowered her head in thought, then said, "Killers never announce themselves. We are in no danger. I have to talk to this woman still."

"But..."

"Please!" Layla was emphatic. She turned back to the woman and said, "Oh, you brought a banner. Please show it to me."

Surprised, Saira—for it was Saira—unfurled the banner. It said, "Allah Never Creates Evil."

"Hmm, very nice, so true," Layla said, looking rather puzzled. She turned back to Saira, who was of her same height. "How can I help?"

"What you said about women went straight to my heart. I was given in marriage to a wealthy older man. I am his second wife, his sex toy. The senior wife lives in the same house with me, and I pity her. I have never loved him. He forces me to wear a niqab and tells me if I don't he'll have me genitally mutilated. You see me wearing only a hijab, like you, and I swear to Allah

I will never wear that monstrosity again. Please tell me what to do, I beg of you. I'm afraid to go home!"

Layla stared at Saira, then looked over at Silas, standing off to the side. She had no idea what to say. "Wait," she said, and closed her eyes and prayed to Allah for guidance. And it seemed to come.

"This is what I would do. Go home, tell him of your resolve, and see what he does. Oh, do you have a job?"

"Yes."

"Is it enough to support you alone?"

"Yes, I think so. If they don't fire me."

"You're not pregnant?"

"No."

"Then this is what I would do. Mind you, this is only what *I* would do. I would go home in my hijab and tell him you're done with the niqab. See what he does. If he yells at you, that's not enough. But if he beats you, leave. Leave at the first opportunity. You shouldn't put up with that. And if he doesn't, but continues to threaten you with a cutting, give him a little time. See if he's serious. If he is, leave. If he's not, if it's just an empty threat, which it probably is—after all, this isn't Somalia—well, then it's up to you what to do next."

"But I'm so miserable. I want to be like you. What can I do?"

"Look. I have to go. Saira, is it?"

"Yes, Saira Marwat."

"Marwat. That's Pakistani, right?"

"Yes, Pashtun."

"Here, I have a card. Call me in a few days if you like, and let me know what happened."

"Thank you! Thank you! I will."

"May Allah keep you safe," Layla said, extending her hand.

Saira bowed reverently with tears in her eyes, picked up her banner, and left.

As Si and Layla walked out of the park behind three policemen, he asked her about the meaning of Saira's banner. "'Allah Never Creates Evil'—how is that a protest?"

"I have no idea," said Layla. "Maybe she's a philosopher."

"Hmm. A strange girl," said Silas.

# Chapter 6

Over the next seven years the world witnessed countless atrocities. The Caliphate had mastered techniques for setting off bombs in the holds of airplanes, and planes had crashed all over Asia, Europe, and the Americas. It had reached a point in the United States where those who could afford it flew in aircraft designed for passengers alone, with their baggage following in separate smaller aircraft, while those who couldn't afford this protection flew with their baggage in the hold. This "solution" created an ugly divide between the rich and the not-so-rich and unparalleled congestion at the nation's airports with all the extra planes. Politicians lost or retained their positions depending on which side they favored. On the nation's highways tunnels became a favorite target for bombers, and huge explosions began showing up on container ships at the nation's ports. One of the more notable calamities occurred in Southern California when the Caliphate scrambled the auto guidance systems along a 200-yard stretch of a freeway. Many injuries and twenty-seven deaths followed.

Europe fared worse, not because of more spectacular cases of butchery, but because of the frequency. Over a five-year period, longevity decreased two-and-a-half years in Germany alone. It was like living in the Middle Ages during the time of plague, with everyone knowing it might be their turn next.

The Middle East fared worst of all, with daily flare-ups between Sunni and Shia the norm. Sunni countries sponsored the radicals, while Shia countries, especially Iran, tried to contain them, not necessarily because they found the radical ideology less persuasive, but because their traditional hatred of the Sunni overcame ideology. In recent years the United States and Iran had even become partners in their fight against a common enemy. The world marched to a course unimaginable twenty years earlier.

With all the death surrounding everyone, death became generally less terrifying. As in centuries past, parents did not presume so quickly that their children would outlive them; for violence was no respecter of age. Religion had become more widespread and more otherworldly, with books on the afterlife not only proliferating, as they had been for a long time, but read by every element of society, from university-educated tycoons to men and women living in homeless shelters and shut away for life in prisons.

Silas, now thirty-two, landed his first tenure-track job at New York University. Yale University Press had published a polished version of his doctoral dissertation in which he laid out the road to peace between Islam and the rest of the world, and NYU had taken notice. But since that success—which seemed purely theoretical since the world was no closer to peace—his interests had turned toward heaven. It became gradually clear to him that the battle would be waged, not on the ground, but in the skies. If Islam was ever going to change, its view of what happened at death would have to change first. And he thought he knew how to make that change happen, he knew where to look—if only Islam would listen. He laid out the map leading to that result in his next book—published not by a university press but by a relatively small press in Britain that catered to informed intellectuals, including, he hoped, Muslims.

The book was very widely read, but mostly by ordinary people interested in what would happen to them at death, not by the world's movers and shakers. His bosses at NYU were not impressed, not even after he pointed out the advantages that a modified, research-based view of the hereafter held for Muslims. The problem was that this "evidence" applied to everybody else as well, including Jews and Christians. And NYU's Religious Studies faculty was mostly a collection of secular scholars who regarded the afterlife as archaic or the stuff of fairy tales. They thought the less talk of an afterlife the better for everyone. And NYU's president, an IBM AI Genius, model 5XQ, was not even conscious. Silas couldn't help suspecting that Harv, the nickname the faculty gave it, was no more objective than the chair; and it certainly had no personal interest in an afterlife. He found himself with no allies and a tenure decision approaching.

In his loneliness he constantly dreamed of Layla, who took a position at the University of Asmaul Husna just a few miles south of him in Brooklyn, where, coincidentally, Saira worked. Silas had had girlfriends, even Catholic girlfriends, even had sex with two of them, but they always left him unsatisfied. He found himself going to bars too often, drinking a little too much, watching too much television. At times he felt almost desperate for a companion, a compatible, loving companion to return home to every evening, in short, a wife. And that meant Layla.

But Layla was a Muslim. Could he become one? He could fake it, but, no.

He and Layla texted frequently and phoned each other once every two weeks or so. They were friends, perhaps even best friends—Si couldn't be sure. Layla was turning thirty in a few days, and he looked forward to being with her on her birthday. He'd catch the subway down to her place in the Clinton Hill area of Brooklyn and take her out to dinner—that much was arranged. There was a great deal more unbeknownst to her that was not.

He found, to his great surprise, Layla and Saira together when he showed up. He gave Layla a light embrace, then turned to Saira.

"Do you remember me?" she said before he could get a word out. "I was that crazy girl who pestered Layla after that talk in Central Park."

"Ah yes, I do. Everything about that time, it'll never go away. It was probably the greatest moment of my life."

"I thought you'd be interested in seeing her," said Layla.

"Now she's not even as much a Muslim as I am. As you can see, she doesn't wear the hijab."

He quickly scanned her as she giggled in sympathy with Layla. From head to toe she was a beautiful woman. He saw she wasn't wearing a ring either.

"But I'm still a believer," she said. "Very much so. But now I know there's more to religion than Islam. I've been taking online courses from all over the place for the last five years. All Muslims ought to be required to take such courses. And do you know what? I actually find Christianity attractive in some respects."

"Perhaps more attractive than I do," joked Si, "and I'm a Christian! But you haven't been tempted to convert?"

"Oh, heavens no."

Layla broke in. "Si, I wonder if we could—if we could bring Saira along with us to—"

"Oh, no, not a chance!" said Saira. "You guys have a lot to talk over, I'm sure. Another time. Hey, I'm off."

*Thank God for that,* thought Si, though on any other day he'd have been glad for her to tag along.

She waved her hand at the door, smiled, and said, "Have fun, you guys!" She swished through the door in her silky black trousers and was gone.

"She's something else," said Si.

"And she's brilliant."

"Is she? And what about that awful man, that husband of hers?"

"He's long gone. That's quite a story."

Si then became quiet and studied Layla. "Happy birthday," he said soulfully as he leaned forward and gently kissed her on the cheek next to the little emerald stud that glistened on her nose. Then he pulled out her favorite perfume from his pocket and gave it to her. "Eau de Medina," he joked.

She smiled. "You didn't have to. But thanks." She unscrewed the top of the tiny bottle and sniffed it. "So where are we off to?"

They walked a few blocks in the cool September air and found a cozy Moroccan restaurant that wasn't too crowded or noisy and sat down. Never much at naming what was right around him, he finally took in her appearance. She wore a red hijab dappled with tiny blue crescents over a dress of rich scarlet. They both ordered a tangine; his was chicken, hers beef.

The food was delicious and the conversation a mix of how they felt about their lives and university politics. After Layla asked for a box to take the uneaten portion of her food home, Silas opened up his heart as never before.

"Layla, what I'm about to say I've run through my mind a hundred times. You are more than a friend. When I hear from you, even just a short, meaningless text, I am happy. I don't have to tell you that I love you, and I suspect the love is returned, at least in some provisional way—you've said as much. Where do we stand? That's what I need to hear from you. Where do we stand *now*?"

Layla came to the point without preamble. "Oh, my dear friend, you know where we stand. Nothing has changed. I would be delighted to be your wife if—if you were a Muslim. I would consider myself a lucky girl, but—"

"But much *has* changed. You're thirty now. You might go through life single. You are not the kind of woman that ordinary guys would find easy to love. This isn't to your discredit; it's to *their* discredit! They aren't capable of seeing what I see if only one has the eyes. I have such eyes, Layla."

"Si, if I have to go through life single and childless, then that's God's will. I accept it. Besides, I'm incredibly busy, with speeches to give one place or another every week. You know, if I wanted to, I could make a living charging for my time. And so could you. Have you ever thought about joining a speaker's bureau? You're a great speaker; you're so cerebral yet so intense, and everyone knows who wrote most of the speech. For all I know, you could be mayor of this city someday."

"Are you serious? All the ideas were yours. I just edited them. Anyway, that's not what you want. You want children. You've dreamed of that, Layla. You've told me that. You count! You count in God's eyes too. Surely God wants you to be happy too."

She looked down at the tablecloth, and Si thought he saw her eyes beginning to moisten. She said nothing.

"In so many ways," he continued, "you're a liberated woman. Muslim men can marry a Christian, but Muslim women can't? You must see the absurdity of that. The unfairness. You don't have to put up with it. And you shouldn't. And in fact many women in your position don't."

"Older women, yes. But not younger women who can bear children. But what does that have to do with us?"

"Come now! Layla, we could raise our children in your faith. You have my word. At some point they would, of course, choose their own way, but we could start them out with—"

"No, Si. You would influence them, even if you didn't try to. Your sons would want to be like you. Maybe not your daughters, but your sons. Besides, I'd lose all credibility with my fellow Muslims if I married a Christian. I'd have no impact on them. I couldn't further the agenda that both of us want."

"Are you sure? Have you thought this through? If you, the revered Layla Haddad, were to marry a Christian, that would set a great example. It would show the world that God smiled on intermarriage between Christian and Muslim. Yeah, many Muslims would hate you for it, but others would love you. It happens all the time anyway, just not between people like you and me. Think it over. You might be missing a great opportunity."

Layla looked steadily at Silas, studied his face, and Silas stared back—the restaurant, the thinning crowd, the stars outside all but forgotten. He could see he scored.

"Layla"—Si's voice rose an octave in his passion for the truth he saw so clearly—"the heroes of our time are those interracial and interfaith couples who place their love above dogma.

Who was it but God who put that love in their hearts? They're setting new standards for the rest of us to live by. They show it's possible for Muslims to live in harmony with non-Muslims. They represent the future, the only way that will ever work. Don't you see—"

"Shut your mouth, you infidel piece of shit!" said a husky voice walking up from behind him. The man had been listening in and now stood to Silas's side. His face was flushed, his eyes full of contempt.

"I beg your pardon," Silas said without getting up.

"I said shut your fucking mouth. You're trying to take this lady to hell with you!"

"No, he's not!" said Layla.

The man acted as if he didn't hear her, as if what she said didn't count. He looked only at Silas and said, "You think interfaith couples are the solution? Why did Allah make such scum as you!"

"Let's go," said Layla in a fluster, grabbing her purse and standing up.

Si got up, glared at the man, and walked to the register to pay the bill.

As they walked home, she asked him if he thought about fighting "that baboon."

He laughed. "How unlike you, my precious, to call a fellow mortal, and a Muslim at that, a baboon."

"He frightened me. I thought there was going to be a brawl."

"Not if I could help it. Besides, he didn't insult you, only me. And I'm used to insults. Only a fool would fight such an imbecile."

Now she laughed. "I didn't know you had such a word for a fellow mortal, my precious!"

He liked that word "precious," even if said in jest. It encouraged him to say more. And for some reason he dared to confess that he "once in a while" slept with other women because he was almost out of his mind desiring a union with her.

"Well," she said, "that's not exactly reassuring. If you can't control yourself before marriage, why should I think you could after?"

"Oh, if only you knew! All it does is tell me over and over that I want no one but you. Fidelity to you would be as natural as... as...as loving the child that God would give us, Layla. You insult yourself by thinking otherwise!"

They walked along without speaking in the gentle night breeze. Then she surprised him by suggesting he "get to know" Saira. "She's a Muslim, but what worthy Muslim would touch her? She wasn't divorced by her husband in the usual Muslim way; she divorced *him* in the American way, the secular way. No Muslim who knows her background would want her in spite of her beauty. She could use a friend, a male friend, a good person like you. The worst of it is that she's seeing a guy who's secular, even claims he's an atheist. Please, do her a favor and get her out of this trap. She is really a great person. And it might take your mind off me."

It almost broke his heart to hear this. If Layla could recommend her best friend to him, there really wasn't any hope. The stars in the clear night sky of Brooklyn that night did not shine on Silas Wyatt.

# Chapter 7

Silas greeted his colleagues in a friendly manner, usually speaking their names when he ran into them on campus. He noticed, however, that they seldom greeted him back by name, and almost never greeted him first. He wondered how he could have offended them, for it was obvious that he had. At department meetings he did his best to fit in, but nothing seemed to help much. His morale worsened when Layla told him over the phone that she was getting married to one of her colleagues where she worked. To make life endurable he called Saira.

One day Saira met him in his office, and they had a rather noisy good time chatting and joking. She came back several times, and it wasn't long before she gained the reputation as "Silas's Muslim girlfriend." When she began sitting in on his graduate-level History of Christian Thought course, not as an enrolled student paying tuition, but as a friend eager to learn, he got into trouble. The Academic Vice President called him in and reprimanded him for violating university rules. "We hired you," she said, "as a model citizen and decorated young scholar. You helped write the 'Deep Shame' speech that's made American history, and we felt incredibly fortunate to attract you to NYU, and to the city where your fame was made. But now this." Silas agreed immediately to exclude Saira from his class and apologized for his naiveté — even though he knew of similar cases that went unnoticed — but a formal reprimand went into his personnel file anyway. Those who might want him fired or not promoted now had a leg up.

A second eruption occurred when he published an article titled "Afterlife of a Suicide Bomber" in *The Washington Post*. What got the attention of his colleagues was not his impressive knowledge of the Quran and Sayings of the Prophet, which spelled out clearly what happens when "martyrs" die. It was his claim that twenty-first century research into paranormal conscious states was a far more trustworthy source. If you want to know what *really* happens to the "martyr," he seemed to be saying, look to science. To make such a claim seemed to his colleagues preposterous, potentially inflammatory, and well beyond the limits of what a Christian theologian with an international reputation had any business saying. This is in part what he wrote:

Before tackling this volatile subject, I should say a word about myself. I'm a professor of Christian and Islamic Studies at New York University with a special interest in afterlife studies. But the speculative presentation you will find here owes nothing to any religion, notably neither to Islam nor Christianity. It comes from deceased persons, or spirits, who communicate to us through mediums, the most authentic that I have identified. These spirits tell us about the world they inhabit—in detail, often at book-length. Many of them discuss suicide and warn against it—as does the Quran: "And do not kill yourselves. Surely, Allah is Most Merciful to you" (4:29).

First, the jihadi, like the rest of us, *will survive,* and he will find himself in a somewhat familiar world, not some "jeweled city, or some monstrous vision of infinity," as one spirit puts it. He will be a spirit among other spirits—and likely not just among any, but among fellow Muslims of his own sect. For there are many sectors in the afterworld, and one is usually greeted and ushered into the afterworld by one's own kind, perhaps one's elder relatives...

Even for the most sincere and innocent of the suicide bombers, there will be no dark-eyed virgins. Instead he will find teachers ready to guide him out of the confusion that led to his murderous deed and premature death. Hating and killing Sunni or Shia or Yazidi or Kurd or Christian or Jew or

Hindu, whatever group he has been taught to hate, will be described, to put a good face on it, as a "miscalculation" — resulting in a crime that the teachers themselves were perhaps guilty of before coming over, and that they are eager to atone for. An especially painful part of the rehabilitation process will be entering into the suffering of the noncombatants he killed. It is even possible that he will meet one of them in person, a harrowing ordeal unless the victim is offering forgiveness. In no way am I writing to disparage the Prophet or the Quran, but to give support to it from an unexpected source. A long life with children and grandchildren to hang on one's neck and kiss one's cheeks should not be given up lightly. Spirit literature shows why life in a human body is precious. It especially warns against suicide and suggests why Allah forbids it and why Muslim warriors have shunned it down through the ages up until now.

But his deadliest mistake occurred in his History of Christian Thought class well after Saira was removed. Now NYU was no bastion of Christianity, far from it. Many Christians, even those living in nearby Brooklyn, avoided it. They found it too Islam-friendly, or too caught up in social issues like Queer Studies, or too Jewish, or too unconcerned with the great metaphysical questions: God, soul, and immortality. For a long time Silas had been convinced that these great questions were being ignored by his colleagues. But there was no way they could go undiscussed in a course like his, and he devised an experiment with his students. "What would the world's greatest Christian thinkers in the ancient world have said if they knew about the Bible what we know about it today?" he asked. "What creed would those three hundred bishops, all men, have formulated in the Greek city of Nicaea in AD 325 if they knew then what we know now?" Silas and his seventeen students, seven of them Christian, had studied the Nicene Creed in detail, and he thought it would be an exciting experiment to turn them into formulators of a more plausible creed with all the advantages of contemporary scholarship—an "updated" creed, he called it. He promised to share his version with them at the end of the experiment. Most of the students were intrigued and excited, and that night they went home, formulated their creeds (in under three hundred words, as Silas required), and mailed them in. Si read their work and was delighted, with one exception: One of the students mailed in the Nicene Creed exactly as the Church fathers had written it.

He then mailed them his own version, but with a final assignment: "How would my creed have changed Christianity's relation to Islam? Think about that, and we'll discuss it when we meet next. Excited? I am!"

Here was Silas' creed:

I believe in God the Father and Mother, creator of the universe. I believe in the teachings of Jesus Christ, whose life was tragically cut short by corrupt men he outspokenly condemned. He was crucified like a criminal under Pontius Pilate, but his spirit did not die. Shortly after his death his closest friends saw him in spirit and took heart that he was, while in heaven, still with them; and they could not contain their joy; and out of that joy grew a young movement that would soon be labeled Christianity. I believe that the same divine spirit in Jesus is in all of us and that the Christian Church exists to help us grow into saints modeled after him. I believe that we are called to forgive each other and strive for justice for all. I believe that life is everlasting and heaven is the ultimate destination for which all men and women were created. Amen.

One of his students showed Silas's creed to the chair, Dr. Paul Karlsson, a Swede in his sixties noted for adopting minority causes, and with half a dozen books to his name, all but one of them forgotten. That one was *A Christianity Without Salvation,* in which he argued that Jesus's personal religion offered salvation in this world only, not in the next. Silas believed that if Christianity ever got reduced to this in the popular mind, Islam's conquest over it was certain, but he hadn't discussed the question with Paul. He suspected, though, that Paul knew how unbridgeable their differences were. Paul called Silas into his office one Wednesday evening after the secretary and her student assistant had gone home.

Silas took his seat and greeted his senior colleague as warmly as he knew how. He noted at once how strained Paul's greeting was.

Paul propped his elbows on the arms of his ergonomic chair and folded his fingers together in front of his chin as he studied his junior colleague—as one might study someone he fears retaliation from. Then he took a troubled breath and sighed. "Silas, you are a young man, and sometimes young men, excellent young men, make a young man's mistake. When a student complains that a professor has required a class to adopt his point of view, I become concerned."

"Yes, I would too," said Silas, now very much on his guard and sensing some kind of ambush, but not guessing where it might be coming from.

"A student sent me your version of the Nicene Creed and said you told the class to write their own version of it, the way they wished it might have been written. Is that correct?"

"Oh, that. Not precisely, but close enough for the moment. Why?"

"She said you didn't allow them to keep the creed just as it was. And she believed it was exactly right the way it was written down eighteen hundred years ago—guided by the Holy Spirit—you know how that goes."

"Well, that's not quite right. I didn't voice an objection against their believing it just as it was written; I only wanted them to make any adjustment they might want to make. It was an experiment, not an effort to indoctrinate. Surely they all knew that."

"That is what you might have intended, but I don't think that is how you came across. I think you required them to provide their own version. And that means something different from the original version."

"Yes, that's right, but, again, not with any intention to indoctrinate. Do you really think I care what they think on the matter?"

"Well, Silas, you certainly didn't make yourself clear. You seemed to be saying, at least to this student, that Christianity needed cleaning up."

"Frankly, I think that every religion needs cleaning up. Don't you?"

"That's not the point. You transgressed on this woman's faith."

"Paul, all I wanted to do was encourage them to think for themselves rather than accept every dogma that comes down the line from antiquity. Whether they do or don't is not my concern. As for the Nicene Creed, I grade them on their knowledge of it, not whether they agree or disagree with it. Most of my students aren't Christian anyway. I just wanted them to get involved and come up with their own critique—to put them back in the ancient world, so to speak. Everyone seemed to greatly enjoy it."

"Except for one of them."

"Yes, that's right." Silas thought it over for a moment, then said, "You have a point. If you'll tell me who the student is, I'll apologize and assure her that I have no problem with her position. It just never occurred to me that—"

"That's the trouble, Silas. According to your colleagues, and now your students, you repeatedly give offense. Things that occur to most people don't seem to occur to you. There is the business about your meeting with women in your office. There is the letting students into your class who are not enrolled and haven't paid any tuition. There is the uproar about your article in *The Washington Post* which brought disgrace to the University."

"Sir, you say 'repeatedly.' None of these things, except for the meetings with my friend in my office, occurred more than once. You've been misinformed. And the so-called woman is a friend and nothing more. She is *not* my girlfriend."

"The fact is, Silas, that your presence in the department is disruptive. Even if the accusations are exaggerated, as I suspected they were, the fact remains that your colleagues cannot work congenially with you and want you removed. It's my responsibility to keep harmony, to keep the machine running smoothly. With that in mind, I've requested the Dean to move you from your present office to an available office in the Econ Department."

Silas heard these words as if they were a death sentence. He loved people and could never understand why some people didn't like him. But his whole department? That was impossible. Did no one in his department speak up for him? He might not have any great friends, but enemies? Enemies without exception?

"Paul, with due respect, I think it's...I think it's...your responsibility to provide justice first, then harmony second. I have never said an unkind word to any of my colleagues. If they don't like me, that's their problem. Or tell me what I have to do, how to apologize for any offense I'm not aware of. Because I think their accusations are absolutely groundless. At least set up a hearing so I can defend myself in front of my accusers."

"Silas, we are required to provide you with an office where you can do your work and students can meet with you. And the Provost has provided this. We are not required to situate you where you would like. You have one week from today to move all your things to the Economics Department. Over on West Fourth Street, Sixth Floor. I'm told it's a nice office. Your phone number will remain the same, and you can take your computer with you. Oh, one thing more: You are not to make contact with your colleagues. You can talk to the secretary, but all communication with them must come through me. You are not even to email them. I'm sorry about this, but it's for the good of the many over the one."

"Paul—" but he didn't know what to say next. He saw with utter clarity that there would be no point in giving a defense. He felt blasted and in shock and could only say, as he rose to go, "You've made a mistake...and more to your shame because you've made your reputation around justice for minorities. I'm a minority of one." As he exited the office, he was boiling.

# Chapter 8

January of 2099 did not bode well for the rest of the year. The Caliphate stepped up its bombing campaign in most of America's big cities, with churches, museums, and monuments the primary targets. Moderate Muslims feared and detested the extremists as much as anyone, but they had not taken to heart the lesson of Central Park that Layla Haddad had challenged them with in her famous speech: to resist the Caliphate boldly, openly, nonviolently, and in great numbers. Other groups did resist, but they did not heed the other part of Layla's message. When the Caliphate entered a church and gunned down worshippers, vigilante groups sworn to protect "the fatherland" gunned down Muslims leaving their mosques. The police prevented nine out of ten attacks before they happened but couldn't prevent them all. But all this paled compared to what happened in Detroit.

Two years earlier a popular Muslim governor won a second term, and violence all over Michigan abated. The state's non-Muslim population, now a minority, learned to trust the new majority and think of them almost as friends. The rest of the country watched hopefully to see if the truce would hold. It seemed to when Detroit elected as mayor a man with dubious but indirect ties to the Caliphate who swore his views had moderated over the years. "I am a man of peace," he declared in every speech he gave, and his good looks and earnest expression seemed to second the claim. But the press became alarmed as they watched his choice of assistants, some of whom they sniffed out as "definitely Caliphate-friendly."

On April 13 the long dreaded "unthinkable" happened: Mayor Mahud Aboud declared sharia as the law of the land, meaning that all Detroit residents, Muslim or not, would have to live by it. And, almost as disturbing, because of its symbolism, the city's new name would be Thlath, or "The Three" in Arabic.

The mayor explained that "The Three" referred to Islam's three holiest cities: Mecca, Medina, and Jerusalem. The governor, expected to condemn the decree in its entirety, condemned only the new name, and Detroit remained Detroit. But he declined to take any further stand "until the ramifications of the decree were fully reviewed."

The nation was in shock as the details of the decree surfaced.

Eight years before, when news of the Central Park Massacre screamed out across the world, Layla called Si for comfort. Si was tempted to call her now, but he resisted. He thought of calling home, but instead he called Saira.

To his surprise, he had managed to get tenure at NYU, perhaps because he was on good terms with the Academic Vice President, a real person and second in command. So now he was an associate professor living on the seventh floor of a faculty residence building looking out over Washington Square. That is where he and Saira agreed to meet—under a 350-year-old elm, battered but still standing, at the northwest corner of the Square. The blustery spring day threatened rain and chill, but they could always retreat to his room—if she would permit it.

She came skipping along smartly with a scarf streaking out behind her. Watching her from a distance, he couldn't help thinking of the lady from Arles in Bizet's famous suite, which he had always loved.

They kissed each other on both cheeks in the French style—a halfway greeting between a hug and a handshake that he had adopted for Saira. The perfect compromise, he thought: the mean between extremes, like the extremes of Christianity and Islam.

Almost before they settled on their bench, she came right to the point. She was seething. "It won't be so bad if they steer clear of sharia Saudi style. But if it's amputation for theft, lashes for drinking alcohol, and death for conversion to another religion, I'll convert to Christianity, I swear I will! I'll court their death. I'll travel to Detroit," she said with a sneer, "and yell to the bastards, 'Come and get me'! Take my head and hang it from the minaret of Dearborn's Great Mosque!" He enjoyed her passion, the deep feeling and wild imagination that were her twin trademarks. How different from Layla, the always wise and dignified love of his life. But he was learning to like this other way of being a woman. He couldn't help chuckling at her.

It did begin to rain, and they did retreat to his apartment. His digs were rather Spartan. The highlight of the living room was a large desk made of a door from Home Depot laid on top of two filing cabinets at either end. Books and papers and class material were spread out over the desk, with sorting trays to the side, both left and right. Behind him was a real desk, an antique given to him by his mother, and on it sat his computer. Between the two "desks" was a swivel chair, so all he had to do to switch from computer to book and back was swing around. It was the perfect solution for a scholar-teacher.

But Si did not want to be a scholar, and teaching students at a university did not have the outreach he wanted. This was the topic that their conversation soon turned to.

He sat at the end of a couch under a strong light used for reading and faced Saira seated opposite on an antique armchair, another gift from his mother. "You know," he began, "I almost regretted the tenure decision. A good old-fashioned skewering would have forced me to do something else. God knows what it would have been. Anyway, here I sit with my books, in my little ivory tower."

"Si, what is this?" she replied in her usual animated style. "Are you being fair to yourself? Your book on the afterlife brings you more mail than you can handle. That's what you told me just a month ago. And the praise it gets on Amazon, my gosh, I wish I had a twentieth the impact with my little talks to women's groups. And that essay on suicide bombers has earned you death threats! What an honor!"

He chuckled again at her way of putting things, always fresh. "You know, Saira, all that attention does help. But email isn't flesh. But let me tell you something about myself you don't know. Once or twice a week I pray with Muslims."

"What? You're kidding! How did that happen?"

"NYU built an interreligious chapel a few years ago, and that's where I go. It's got pews for Christians and Jews, yoga cushions for Hindus and Buddhists, and marked-off prayer spaces for Muslims. I'm usually alone, and that's the way I like it. But if there is anybody else, you can bet it'll be a Muslim."

"So you pray together just like it's natural. That's wonderful. But why not just pray in your apartment?"

"For some reason I like sacred space, space set aside. It makes it easier. It helps me concentrate."

"This is surprising. I didn't know you put much stock in prayer. What do you pray for?"

"As you know, I can't figure out what to do with my life, and I ask God for help. Ask over and over. But so far no answer. No answer. But it feels good to ask, to enquire. And there's a second reason. Deep down I'm lonely, with no colleagues to talk shop with, or enthuse about our best students with, or even ask about their wife or husband and kids at home. Saira, I love people, but life has cursed me with a personality that puts people off. So God has become my companion. All my theological training, and I don't even know who God is. Yet he is my companion. Is he love? I do hope so, and I talk to him like he is. 'Come, Master, come, and fill me wholly with thyself.' That's my favorite prayer. Actually it's attributed to Rumi, a Muslim — do you know Rumi?"

"No, should I?"

"Absolutely. Anyway, I don't pray as a Christian or as a theologian. I'm just a hungry soul looking for a calling. What's the gift I can give to the world that's worthy of me at my best? I haven't found it yet. So I don't have a calling or a true friend. Just fans from all over the world I never get to meet."

With eyes moist, Saira got up from her chair and sat down on the couch. Her knees in pants silky and navy blue pointed at him. "But you do have a friend, Si. Don't doubt that. I didn't know much about your religious life until now. I thought it was a formality, and I didn't respect it. But it turns out you're like me. Just you and your God, an outcast with no one who understands you. Thrown out of the club." She looked at him with her gorgeous eyes, and Si wondered if she had feelings for him. But with her usual unpredictability, she came back to an earlier point, and with a flare that almost made him jump. "Did anyone ever tell you that you look like shit at times?"

Shocked and hurt, he said simply, "No." What else could he say?

"I mean that when you're angry or distressed over something, you have an expression that's, well, menacing. It's scary, intimidating. But" — now her own expression was sweetened by a smile — "when you're your usual amiable or, even better, vulnerable self, you're adorable. Like now." Impulsively she slid over next to him and kissed him on the mouth.

Silas was thunderstruck and instantly aroused, and he grabbed her and squeezed her to him in an awkward sideways sort of way.

"Jeez, Silas, I thought until now I might be a lesbian! It's been a long time since I felt anything for a man. Over seven years."

# Chapter 9

Connor al-Anzi came from a Saudi father and Christian mother who made Detroit their home from the time he was three. Raised to think that the Sunni religion of his father and the Methodist religion of his mother were compatible, he was appalled by the events of 4/13, as the locally imposed sharia on Detroit was called by the media. One day late in Ramadan during the sunset prayer, with his head bent to the floor in adoration of Allah and aching from the exhaustion of hunger, he heard a voice. He took it to be the voice of Allah, and the next day he skipped work and began working on his "manifesto," as he called it. Its eventual title would be "Manifesto for a United Detroit."

The *Detroit Free Press,* a minority source of news still under the control of non-Muslims, published the manifesto not only digitally but in a unique poster version, even though it feared for young Connor's life. Not since the imposition three months earlier had anyone claiming to be Muslim spoken out so boldly in its columns. The editors were privately gleeful and hoped the printed version would be posted all over the city.

After listing the many virtues of Islam that would lead to a "better America," al-Anzi concluded his essay by calling for the following "reforms":

(1) Look to the Quran as a work of divine inspiration but without insisting on its infallibility, (2) look to the Quran and Hadith for guidance, but respect the wide variety of interpretation that comes from their reading, (3) affirm the greatness of the Prophet Muhammad, but do not raise him to Allah's status as an infallible oracle, (4) never require a non-Muslim to follow our sharia, for such a requirement would nullify humanity's free will, Allah's greatest gift to us all, (5) affirm the Greater Jihad which calls on each of us to fight the

demons within our own hearts, but reject the Lesser Jihad that calls for the persecution of infidels as our enemy, (6) do not spread the faith of Islam by force or violence or conquest, but by respectful discussion and noble example, (7) adopt a more forgiving morality in keeping with God's name, "the Merciful," that recognizes the universality of human failing, equally in imam, mullah, man, and woman, (8) recognize that men and women, different in so many ways, as Allah intended, are equals in his eyes and enjoy the same rights and privileges, (9) respect Islam's sister religions as legitimate paths to salvation and renounce the Caliphate's claim to be the only religion approved by Allah, (10) accept criticism from alien perspectives as a show of strength and self-confidence, recognizing that Allah does not need the help of finite beings to defend his honor.

On a warm Friday evening in the middle of July of the year 2099, the Detroit Tigers would be playing a home game against the Chicago White Sox. Game time was 7:10 p.m. But at noon of the same day, temporary gallows were erected on the outfield grass just behind second base. Every Friday afternoon Hakim Hamza Stadium, "the Double H," was turned into a temporary execution site.

Next to the gallows a sword lay on the green turf in gleaming collusion with the sun, which blazed forth under a cloudless sky. The stadium was roughly half full: men outnumbered women twenty to one, with women segregated in their own seating section high above third base. "Execution" was a spectacle that many young men preferred to NASCAR, where speeding cars driven by real humans provided the entertainment. Death was far more certain at the Double H.

Most of the offenders were drug dealers. A few were murderers who couldn't raise enough blood money to gain pardons from the families of the victims. Thievery was usually punished by lashes or amputation of a finger or hand at the central police station, but in aggravated cases hanging was the sentence. Three of the criminals were of this kind. As for the gleaming sword, it was reserved for the unusual crime, and almost everyone in the crowd knew what that meant on this given day.

After a prayer, the proceedings got under way. Twenty-seven were scheduled to die. This included four women, all convicted of murder—three had murdered their bosses, the fourth a child in her care. As colorful flags fluttered from poles surrounding the stadium, and the felons were led one by one to the platform, an official read out the name of the malefactor and the crime he or she had been convicted of. Following that, the rope was slipped over the head and around the neck, and the prisoner had a chance to say a final word. Usually it was "Allahu Akbar" or "Salam alaikum," but occasionally one would yell out he was innocent in a voice resonating with sincerity. On such an occasion the usual quiet was disturbed by an uneasy collective murmur that crept through the stadium like a light breeze before a threatening storm.

The last criminal was of a special kind. This was obvious when no less than the city's vice mayor stepped up to the mike and pulled out a speech from his suit pocket. As he prepared himself, the crowd noticed the hangman move away from the platform and stand next to the sword laid out on the grass. The vice mayor began:

This last criminal, Connor al-Anzi, wrote an article that most of you have probably read. He published it in the city's kafir newspaper, a special edition. Do not be deceived, he is a zindiq, a heretic; and our leading imam, Yassin Mahar, has delivered the fatwa: death by the sword. Now, we are a magnanimous people. We tolerate dissident opinions. But we do not tolerate hypocrites. This man conceals his infidelity while claiming to be a Muslim. In his so-called manifesto he asks us to "accept criticism from alien perspectives as a show of strength and self-confidence, recognizing that Allah does not need the help of finite beings to defend his honor." Do not be seduced by this argument. When we condemn this man to death, it's not to protect Allah from apostates like him, but to protect the common people from his seductions. We are the protectors of Islam, and his opinions lead people astray and corrupt Islamic society. They are attacks on true religion and result in the destruction of the state. But Allah tells us to be merciful. And we were. Over and over we asked al-Anzi to repent, and over and over he declined. The man you see before me has no interest in spreading Islam across the world. He is content to let it stand next to the other religions as if they were all equals. This, as you all know, is not Allah's will. Nor is it his will to allow this man to poison the minds of the uneducated and gullible any longer. But even now we give him one more chance. Connor al-Anzi, do you renounce the heretical views expressed in your so-called Manifesto?

The vice mayor faced the condemned man and waited as the crowd held its breath. Five seconds passed in silence. Then he nodded to the executioner, who picked up the sword. Neither of the men asked al-Anzi if he had any final words. But the condemned man yelled out in a loud voice anyway: "Down with the Caliphate! I am a Muslim!" Another quick nod of the head from the vice mayor. A single powerful swipe of the sword. Connor al-Anzi's head fell to the turf as blood spurted from the neck.

Sitting apart in their respective sections, Silas and Saira witnessed the execution. Silas had come to witness history. He hoped to sell an article describing the grisly event to the *New York Times*.

On the flight home Saira told him she now understood her life's mission.

# Chapter 10

On the afternoon of the next day, Silas was working in his university office on the article. Years earlier, the *Times* had written a long, positive review of his first book on the Islamic question and had reached out to him for comment on later occasions. Silas was on their radar. So when he called them Friday afternoon on the flight home and told them he had just attended the al-Anzi execution in Detroit and wondered if they would be interested in his impressions, they jumped at it. The feature editor told him they'd need it by Saturday evening and that it might be headlined in the Sunday edition. "So get to work, Mr. Wyatt," he said. "You've got about twenty-eight hours."

Silas had about five hours to deadline when the phone buzzed. He almost didn't answer, but he needed a break and was sure it would be either Saira or his mother. So he clicked on. But the voice belonged to a male. It asked if he was the author of the book *Afterlife: The Evidence.*

Exasperated that he'd answered, he said, "Yes, I am."

"A few days ago my wife begged me to call you."

"Oh, what about? Who is this?"

"It doesn't matter. What are you doing in your office on a Saturday afternoon anyway?"

"I'm writing an article and have a deadline. I'm afraid I don't have time for this."

"Please excuse the rudeness. I'm not quite myself. I have a revolver next to me, and I need to know what you might say on suicide. I'm an entrenched atheist and think all talk of a soul is superstition, but my wife insisted that I at least call you. She had read your book."

"A revolver? Do you plan to—?"

"If you hadn't answered the phone, I'd be dead right now. I was sure you wouldn't. But I decided to give the miracle a chance."

*Shit!* Silas yelled inwardly. He had a deadline, and now this. He knew there was no quick way out of it. *Shit, shit, shit!* But he didn't doubt for a second that he had to help. "Can you put the revolver away for little while?" he said.

There were a few seconds of quiet, then a weak "Okay." Silas heard a drawer open and shut.

"Does your wife know what you're thinking of doing?"

"Oh, hell no! But she thinks I'm not prepared to die, just in general."

"Did she tell you anything about what's in the book?"

"Only that we do survive death. That there is an afterlife."

"Can you tell me your name and a little about yourself? I don't have much time though."

"Ethan Drayton. I doubt it'll mean anything to you, but it might. I'm the CEO of a large investment firm. I'm married to a woman who loves my money more than me. I lost my only son to suicide a few months ago. I look out at the world with all its horrors and see it getting worse by the day. And now I suffer from acute bursitis in my hip that affects my golf game. There's a lot more, but I think you get the picture."

"Any money problems?"

"Hardly." He snorted a cynical sort of laugh. "So, can you give me a logical reason why I shouldn't blow my brains out?"

"I think I can. Look, can we talk tomorrow? I can give you a reason to live. I promise. Where do you live?"

"Nearby. Greenwich, Connecticut."

"Can you by any chance meet me in my office tomorrow afternoon?"

"I could. But I'm not sure it'd be worth your time."

"Well, I'm sure it would be worth yours. But before you come, get a copy of my book. Read as much as you can. Chapter 5 if nothing else. Can I expect you?"

They arranged to meet the next day at 3:00 p.m. in his university office.

"Jesus, you're just a kid!" said Ethan Drayton when Silas met him at the flyover dock on the roof of the new Arts and Sciences Building. Drayton's shiny black vehicle gleamed under the sun. The building was deserted.

"Did you see the article in the *Times* this morning on the execution?" Silas said on the elevator down to the first floor.

"Yeah, just one more reason to check out of this sick world. The Caliphate will run the country in twenty years. Those goddamn fuckers!"

"I'm not so pessimistic. But even if they did...anyway, I, uh, wrote the article."

"You wrote the article? The article in the *Times*?" He studied Silas in disbelief.

"Yes, I really did. I was at the execution."

"In Detroit?!"

"Yep."

"You write for the *Times*? Your last name's—Christ, I've forgotten!"

"Wyatt. Silas Wyatt."

"How old are you?"

"Thirty-four."

"Same age as my son. Damn!"

Once settled in his chair, the same Saira sat in, Ethan told Silas he was a graduate of Wharton, on his third marriage ("the best of the lot, but not by much"), a recovering alcoholic who had been dry for fifteen years, a successful "manipulator" of stock derivatives ("but entirely legal"), and was now sixty-three and at the top of his career. Even after his only son died, his resolve never to drink had not faltered. He had an immaculately cropped gray beard and shaggy eyebrows that hung incongruously over his wide-set eyes. His face was reddish and slightly blotched, his belly somewhat swollen from a daily diet of half a dozen Pepsis. He owned a forty-four-foot sailboat that he once enjoyed sailing in Long Island Sound and was a member of the Winged Foot Golf Club. Silas could tell the man was loaded.

"It scared the crap out of me," he began when the conversation turned to the book. "I read your Chapter 5 and saw that I was trapped. Trapped to go on living. I physically had the sense that the couch I was sitting on was in freefall through space, turning slowly, with me still sitting on it. You convinced me that killing myself would be cowardly and none of my problems would go away. It would only make new problems for others, especially my daughters and their families. It frightens me to think how close I came! I would have landed in a hell of remorse, self-inflicted and without any immediate remedy. I owe you a lot."

"Your guardian angel must have been working overtime. Do you know how slim the chances were that I'd be working in my office on a Saturday afternoon?"

"It gives me goose bumps to think of it!" He stood up and started pacing. "It was amazing, but your book almost made me wish I was religious. I couldn't believe it. But even if there is a God, I don't like the bastard much. My goddamn brain can't manufacture enough serotonin to keep me wanting to live another day. So now I'm hooked on antidepressants, 50 milligrams a day. That's a high dose. I've got two great daughters, a job that anybody else would kill for, a few good friends, a mansion with nine bedrooms, and I'm so miserable without Serozac I couldn't live without it. And it seems like every woman over fifty I know is on the stuff. Life is just plain godawful painful. And now I have to get up and pee every two hours during the night because my prostate is swollen. It amazes me how I got through Tyler's death in one piece."

"Well, it seems to me," Si said, "what you have to do is find a reason to live. A reason worthy of you. And of the Source—God, if you will—who, I believe, made you. That won't be easy. But with all your money it won't be especially hard either. Let me ask you this. What are you good at? What is your God-given talent?"

"God-given talent? Making money, I guess. Making money for myself and my clients who already have too much. They come from all over the world. That's my talent. You might even call me a genius at making money. But what is that worth?"

"Plenty. Think of all the good you can do with all that money."

"Let me tell you something. I give tons away every year. I'm a sucker for every sob story. But making a donation on my computer takes about ten seconds. And now there's not even any more golf. And the kids would rather sail with their friends than their old man. And my wife is—but don't get me started on that subject! I just don't know what to do with all the time I have except make more money."

"I don't mean to be insulting, but I want to put your sufferings in perspective. Do you know how your complaints would sound to a Somali mother whose children are starving?"

"Goddammit, do you want to add to my shame? Of course, I know! But how dare you lecture me? You have no idea what it's like to be me? You're just a puppy!"

"Sorry. You're right, I don't." Silas shriveled under the man's wrath. He had never come across such power in a human being. Ethan Drayton was all CEO.

"You're goddamn right you don't! Anyway"—he stopped pacing and sat back down in his chair—"I'm more principled than you think. I was ready to do what weaker men only think about. And my eyes are wide open to what's happening in the world. I read widely. Hmm, Silas Wyatt. That name suddenly rings a bell. Did you write...did you write that book on the Islamic question that was praised so widely, and that I found, sorry, so naïve?"

"That was me. And now I think it was naïve too."

"Hell, how many books *have* you written?!"

"Just two. How about some more water?"

"Thanks. The doctor says to drink water every chance I get."

Si got up to get the water and called back over his shoulder, "What did you mean by being more principled than I think?"

"Forget it. The point is you convinced me to stick around." He paused. "Call me Ethan, if you like."

"Okay. And call me Si."

The older man suddenly brightened and said, "How'd you like to go sailing? We could talk over what's worth doing in the few years I've got remaining. And maybe I could teach you how to invest your money."

"What money? I'm a professor!" Si joked. "Sailing. That would be nice. Hmm. Yeah. Thanks. Oh, could I bring a friend? A lady friend?"

"Sure. But I won't be bringing my wife."

"That's all right. Yeah. I like the idea. And maybe you can teach me the difference between starboard and—what's its opposite?"

# Chapter 11

Silas walked through the door of the fifty-two-story New York Times Building at the heart of Manhattan. He admired the cherrywood walls and red velvet seating of the auditorium that looked out at the shiny white birch trees in the atrium. Though nearly a hundred years old, the building, both interior and exterior, had a freshness that one might find in a Shinto shrine built new every twenty years. He remembered that this was the site of a detonation by a suicide bomber four years ago. One would never guess it.

He took an elevator up to the eleventh floor and found a secretary waiting for him.

"You must be Silas Wyatt. Welcome to the *Times!* Have a seat, and I'll notify the boss you've arrived," she said.

Stan Liggett, vice president of the *Times,* appeared with a big smile and warmly outstretched hand. "Hello, Silas. We're waiting for you, eager to meet you." Stan led Silas into a nearby conference room. "Ladies and gentlemen, meet Silas Wyatt."

Fourteen men and women—a mix of editors and columnists and two vice presidents, evenly divided between the sexes—nodded friendly faces toward him. "Here, have a seat." Silas was directed to the seat at the head of the long table. Stan took his seat at the opposite end.

After the introductions, Stan got down to business. "Silas, I take it you know some of these notables"—he laughed good-naturedly at them—"at least by their columns. As I told you over the phone, we are considering luring you away from NYU and adding you to our stable of OpEd columnists. I gather you've thought this over. We've been impressed by the guest columns you've written for us and for others, but, of course, we do have questions. And no doubt you have questions of us. But first, would you like to join our staff? Or would you prefer to stay on at NYU?"

Silas, dressed in a coat and tie, and fresh from a haircut at the local barber's—he usually cut his own hair with a shaver he bought at Walmart—remembered what Saira told him about his menacing frowns and had practiced in the mirror how to mitigate the problem. To say that he was nervous would be an understatement. He began: "First, let me say how honored I am to meet you all. I would very much like to work as a columnist for the *Times* and would happily resign my position at NYU if the conditions were right. I do have tenure, however, and I know you don't give tenure." He smiled, and they laughed. "It would be enough for me to feel I occupied a meaningful niche. And feel free to call me Si."

"Thank you, Si. Well, first I should explain that opinions in this room run the gamut, especially on the Islam question, and you won't be able to please us all. But a meaningful niche you would certainly fill. We've gone from not one religion editor before 2030 to at present three, each representing a different specialty. What we like about you is your broad perspective, your ability to navigate around and through them all, especially Christianity and Islam. Of course, you would be able to write on whatever subject you liked. But the religious question would, presumably, be your primary focus."

A half hour into the interview a woman dressed in a sari asked Si what he knew about Islam's treatment of Hindus and Sikhs in India.

"Enough to know where to look for the details," he said.

"Without going into the details, can you tell us in a general way if you see Islam as a religion of peace?"

Silas knew instantly that the way he handled this question would dictate his fate. This, after all, was the great question that no doubt divided not only the people in the room but the entire world. He braced himself and began: "Historically, Islam has been a religion of peace for Muslims and a religion of conquest for everyone else. This has been especially true for India, where Hindus were given the choice to convert or die, and where their temples were destroyed by the thousands because they were dedicated to false gods. No one who knows history can deny this. The conquerors themselves boasted of their plunder, all carried out in Allah's name; they tell of it in their own histories. But we all know this, don't we? The trouble is we're afraid to call it by its right name: not a religion of peace, but of conquest. But then there is the other face of Islam, or rather faces, and they have a different story to tell, a completely different story, and sometimes a beautiful one, one that deserves to endure and will endure. Bridging the gap between these various Islams is what I'll be writing about. Getting the names right, not just of the past, but of the present, is crucial."

"Thank you. That's reassuring," said the woman.

"Not to me," said a man whose dress identified him as a Muslim, and who stood up as he spoke. "I am Amir al-Shami. Sir, Islam does have many faces, but what troubles me is your first choice. Why not begin by saying today's Islam is a religion of peace, and then get around to the past and the other Islam? But you began by saying it was a religion of conquest. Your choice suggests a bias."

Silas had read al-Shami's columns from time to time and admired the great skill with which he advanced the cause of his religion. But Silas was certain al-Shami looked to the day, however distant, that Islam would cover the earth in total conquest. He understood his critic. Still, it was a difficult question, not at all one he had anticipated. He paused for a few seconds and gathered his thoughts. Then, "Well, as I see it, a columnist doesn't write about peace, but conflict. We try to create peace, sure, but we don't write about it. We analyze conflict, then try to diminish or remove it, sure, but once we have had our say, we move to the next conflict. We always begin with conflict. That's the way our minds work. I think you would agree that the attempt to conquer innocent people creates conflict. And that's why I started with conquest. It doesn't imply bias. It's just the way our minds work."

Al-Shami stood as if transfixed for a second or two while everyone stared at him. Then he smiled, lightly clapped his hands, and sat down. Silas was surprised and puzzled. Had he made a friend, or was he being mocked? Either way, he was happy with his defense. He could tell the others liked what he said.

After fifty minutes of being grilled, the tone shifted. "Si," said the international affairs columnist Caleb Smith, "if you could do anything in the world, what would it be? I mean, you obviously didn't find professoring especially to your liking, but is there anything you'd rather do than write a column?"

"Great question," Silas replied with a delighted smile. If he'd suspected he was among any but the best and brightest minds in the business, he'd have replied more cautiously. Instead he said, "Yeah, my first choice would be politics."

"Really? And at what level?"

"Oh, I don't know. Maybe as mayor of Schenectady or something."

"Here here!" said one of the women. "He can even pronounce the word. I never could."

"You've got to aim higher than that," said one of the other guys, for "guys" is what they had suddenly become.

"Well then, maybe governor—governor of Alaska maybe. I like Alaska."

"No no! That'll never do," said Caleb. "Their capitol building doesn't even have a dome. It looks like a weather-beaten six-story hotel. You've got to aim higher than that." Everybody was now having fun.

"Okay, how about mayor of New York?"

"Now you're talking," said Caleb.

After it was all over, the columnists took Silas out to lunch and plied him with a martini. *Watch out,* he thought. He remembered how frisky he could get with just one beer.

And he did get frisky. He told the Hindu woman how much he liked her sari. He said he preferred the beautiful colors of a sari to the "drab blacks and whites" of the usual business suit of the Western woman. And then he noticed one of his companions wearing just such a suit and a rather forced smile.

Had he won them over at the interview? Except for the blunder over lunch, he thought he did well. But he dared not get his hopes up. But oh! To be counted among the world's most gifted pundits! To have a job requiring him to write two essays per week for an audience, not of thirty-five college students, but of a hundred thousand readers who moved and shook the world! To have colleagues not composed of petty intellectuals but of men and women who knew his worth and paid him for it! And to be able to work at home except for Fridays when everybody had to come into work. The thought of going back to NYU suddenly became unbearable. He could move anywhere within a hundred miles of New York; he could afford a bungalow in the woods of Western Connecticut or a small apartment looking out over the Hudson. And he could tell his persecutors to go screw themselves.

He decided to walk all the way home just to air out his exhilaration—for he really did think he would get the call. They seemed to like him. If only he hadn't made that idiotic remark about women's apparel! *Holy shit!*

# Chapter 12

Sure enough, Ethan Drayton called and offered to take Silas sailing. "Silas the sailor," he joked on the phone after Silas took him up on the offer.

"And I'll be bringing my lady friend, if that's all right."

"Absolutely. And if Maddy behaves herself, I'll even bring my wife. A little distaffular ambience never hurt."

"Distaffular? I don't know that word."

"Never mind, you won't find it in a dictionary. Anyway, we'll go out on the Sound. It's not supposed to be too hot."

Maddy and Ethan looked at Saira with great interest when she came out of the bathroom in her bathing suit. A sleek royal blue leotard covered her from neck to ankles. Over it a sleeveless fuchsia shirt hung down to her upper thighs. Their social circles did not include Muslims, but her beauty was such that her religion could be excused. They pretended that nothing was out of the ordinary.

"This is a *ship!* You actually own this?" Saira said. She wore a floppy wide-brimmed tennis hat Ethan found for her.

"I do. Would you like to learn how to sail it?"

"Well, I guess. But maybe I should leave that up to you and Si."

"Not at all!" Maddy chimed in. She looked about forty, was evenly tanned all over her body, and had long hair as light as flax. She wore a skimpy black bikini with an unbuttoned lime-colored shirt draped over her shoulders. Both she and Saira were beautiful women, but as different as the Taj Mahal from an Anglican cathedral. "What a man can do, a woman can do twice as well. You know that!" she joked.

Saira didn't much like the joke but smiled anyway.

Ethan and Si wore baggy old bathing suits that looked like

castoffs from Goodwill. Ethan wore a stained orange golf shirt with the collar turned up, while Si settled for a white T-shirt. Each wore baseball hats.

The wind blew briskly out of the southwest under a mostly cloudy sky. The Sound was choppy with whitecaps, and the boat sped ahead under full sail.

"Saira, come on up and take the helm," Ethan said. "It's not like a car. You get to steer it."

Standing side by side, Ethan's curiosity got the best of him. "I think it's the first time I saw a bathing suit like yours without the hijab."

"Yeah, they make them this way, but you're right. Most of them come with a hijab."

"So, if it's not too indiscreet, may I ask why yours doesn't?"

"It's not at all indiscreet," Saira said. "If you're not curious, you might as well be dead!"

*A true Saira-ism,* Si thought as he looked on with amusement.

"The reason I don't wear it is that it hides a woman's beauty, and in my religion that's a sin."

"But you're a Muslim, right?"

"Yes."

"I thought Muslims, observant Muslims, thought that *revealing* a woman's beauty was a sin."

"It's not quite that simple. Anyway, I'm not what you'd call an observant Muslim."

"Turn the wheel to port, Saira, to the left...No, not so much... There, that's better." Then Ethan looked over at Si and said, "Port, that's the word you were looking for the other day, as in starboard *and port.* Remember?"

"Ah, yes."

Ethan turned back to Saira. "So what do you call a non-observant Muslim like yourself?"

"Some would call me a heretic. But I think of myself...I don't know."

"How about lukewarm, like the Christians I know?"

"Oh no! That would be a mistake. I just think for myself, that's all."

"Believe me, that was not meant as an insult. Lukewarm is what I am, at best. After reading Si's book, I don't know what to believe."

"For him that's progress," Maddy said.

The four of them sat near the back of the boat under an awning over the cockpit.

"We're going to tack, so watch the boom and hang on," said Ethan. "We'll heel to port for a while." He performed the maneuver, then said, "Si, would you take the helm? I'd like to talk to Saira. Just head in the direction of that tower way over there."

"Sure." Silas stood up and took the wheel.

"Saira, I'm truly curious. What do you get out of your religion? I mean, does Islam bring you happiness?"

Before Saira could answer, Maddy jumped in. "The impression I have is that Muslims don't know how to have fun. Every day, even in the worst heat, a woman wearing a burqa walks by our house with, I guess it's her husband, getting their exercise. That can't be fun."

Si looked down at Saira just waiting for her to pounce. She was never bested when seemingly cornered.

"Well, I'm not for the burqa. But I might be enjoying life as much in that burqa as in this boat. I mean, how much fun are we really having? I think of fun as a cheap form of happiness. Islam doesn't bring much fun, but it can bring a lot of happiness."

"How so?" said Ethan.

"I can only speak personally. I look around me and what do I see? Every kind of addiction: drugs, alcohol, video games, texting, gambling, pornography, bad music, overeating, luxury, even sports. We look at celebrities and rich people and envy them. We think we have to have what they have or we can't be happy. But what is their life really like? They go from one diversion to the next, and each diversion is over and done with in a day. So the next day they crave another diversion, and it's over and done within an hour. Then what? It's just a matter of time before the diversions give out, and then they're miserable. But God isn't like that. He's always with us. We look within and there he is, and we don't crave what the world has to offer. Nothing can make me happier than knowing I'm doing what Allah approves of and that he approves of me. Nothing can bring me more peace than that. And the Quran shows me what he approves of."

"I don't know, Saira," said Ethan. "That sounds like an awful lot of work to me, and not much pleasure to show for it...Silas, come around to starboard about fifteen degrees more."

"But in all honesty," said Maddy, "let's face it. All those diversions, as you call them, are what make life fun, or at least bearable. You just have to have enough of them. I have enough to keep me occupied all day long, from my lipsticks to my facials to my workout routines to my novels to television to texting my friends, a long list of them. Isn't that what normal people have? It seems to me you're in denial about that."

"If that's good enough for you, then I guess it'll have to do. It's just that we don't agree about what's best for ourselves."

"It just seems to me," said Ethan, repeating himself, "that it's just a godawful lot of brutal inner work."

"It is," said Saira. "And that's what makes life so great. We can never be bored if we challenge ourselves. That's the true jihad, the war we wage within ourselves, the inner struggle. There is always something to do, something important. There is no end to the ways we can make ourselves a better person. And it does require work, brutal work, as you say. But the struggle lasts only a lifetime. Then we go home to God and experience Eternity. And that is the mother of all lesser happinesses. What a destiny! Don't you agree?" She leveled a stare at Ethan that left him momentarily speechless, as if he were being confronted by someone who actually thought he might be capable of such a thing.

"I've got to go pee," said Maddy. She disappeared into the cabin.

"Well," said Ethan, "this doesn't sound much like the Islam that's in the news. But I have to give it to you. You are one hell of an amazing girl."

"Not really. I'm just an ordinary Muslim."

Silas quietly looked on with a smile and said, looking at Ethan, "Don't believe that. She's the kind of Muslim that could change the world."

A little later Ethan anchored the boat in a cove, and they all, with souls so varied, went for a common swim in the chilly but refreshing water of Long Island Sound. It was then that Silas told Ethan about the job interview he'd had at the *Times*.

On the way home, seated side by side in their cab, Silas and Saira shared their impressions of the afternoon.

"I really liked Maddy," said Saira.

"Maddy? You're kidding. Who could be more opposite from you?"

"I like all those things too. I just didn't admit it. I should have."

"Yeah, but that's all she has. You have that and so much more."

"Those little things make me happy too, Si. They really do. I'm not some great spiritual warrior, though I want to be. I even wish you hadn't hired the cheapest pod you could find. I'd have been willing to help out. You see? I like nice things."

He remembered he'd turned off his phone and pulled it out of his pocket. "Do you mind?"

"I do mind. I want your full, undiluted attention!" she joked. "Go ahead."

He switched it on and immediately saw there was a message from Stan at the *Times*. "Saira, look!"

"What? Oh my God!"

"Well, let it be recorded. We are riding in the most dilapidated pod in—where are we?"

"New Rochelle."

"And it's 8:13 p.m., July 16, 2099. And the entire future of my life is about to be announced. I'm thirty-four years old."

"He's probably just going to tell you to call him."

"Well, let's see. Do you want to give the odds?"

"Odds? Oh, yes. Sixty percent yes, sixty percent you call him back or he'll call you later."

"What about no?"

"Minus twenty percent."

"Well, here goes."

She leaned her shoulder against his and peeked.

They read together, *Congratulations, Silas. You got the job. Call me tomorrow. Stan.* "I don't believe it!" Silas said in a voice full of amazement.

"Wonderful! Wonderful!" said Saira. "I am so happy for you, Si. But I expected it. What I can't believe is that I am now sitting next to a big shot." And she laughed in delight.

"A big shot, eh? Hey, that makes two in one day."

"What do you mean?" she said.

"Ethan is a big shot."

"Oh."

"Saira, I can't believe this is happening. I really can't."

When they arrived at Saira's apartment back in Brooklyn, she invited him up. It would not be the first time he'd been in her apartment—he'd come by to pick her up a few times before—but it was the first time she invited him in.

They sat for a little while side by side and drank lemon water.

"It's almost as if," he said, "I'd turn on the TV and there would be an announcement of this great event."

She was uncommonly mellow and snuggled up against him just a little, more than she ever had before. He was touched and excited.

Then she said the thing that made the day even more eventful. "Si, I love you. Do you know that?"

He looked down at her and held his breath.

"Kiss me," she said.

He did, and kissed her again, and again, until his hand, with a mind of its own, ran down her leg dressed in the usual silky pants, crimson this time.

She didn't stop him, and he then ran his hand up along her thigh. And she became almost a beast in her passion.

"Come," she said, and she led him into the bedroom.

"Take your shoes off," she said, as she took off her own.

They lay on top of her small single bed that in all its history had never held a man.

He helped her lift off her light cotton shirt, then unsnapped her bra. His state of mind was dreamy but concentrated. He proceeded slowly to give her a chance to change her mind.

"Si, I haven't been with a man since my marriage. I'm a reconsecrated virgin. Do you love me?"

"Yes. I do. But do you love me?"

"Yes."

"Are you sure?"

"Yes! Yes!" And she began to slide off her pants.

"I want you to promise me one thing," she said. "No penetration. I'm not protected. I want to stay a virgin. I promised God I would until I married. But I'll see to it that you're satisfied." She left her panties on. They were white and not designed to be sexy.

"Okay."

Then she undid his belt and asked him to strip down to his underwear.

"Okay," he said submissively. He was incredibly excited, more than he could ever remember.

For a while they held each other and kissed, but then she sat up and turned him over on his back. She slid his underwear off and began to apply her lips to—

"No, no," he said. "Come here." He knew he couldn't hold out for more than seconds. He pulled her down beside him.

They kissed without speaking and rubbed hard against each other. It was clear to him that she was wild with passion, almost out of her mind. She started reaching down to her panties as if she would pull them down but restrained herself. Again she did this, and again, until she almost ripped them off and tossed them aside. "Now be careful she said. Be careful."

Now he touched her clitoris, and began rubbing, but suddenly she pushed his hand away and turned her body close against his. And she began to move up and down against him. There was nothing separating them now except willpower. He let her move up and down while striving to prevent penetration, up and down until it happened. She heaved out a great ecstatic sigh as he slipped in. And within seconds he was done. There was no stopping it.

Both lay still and pondered what had happened.

"I never knew," she said, "what it was like until now. True love. Wonderful love. I never knew. May God forgive me."

"Not with your husband? Not ever?"

"No. Nothing like this. With him it was always work. I did it for Allah because it was my duty."

"And now?"

"There are no words." Then she grew solemn. "What are we going to do?"

"I don't know. Now you've made love out of wedlock, and to a Christian. That's two death penalties for the same act according to the Caliphate."

"Yes it is, and for some reason I feel Allah has blessed me even though I broke my vow. But what will I feel tomorrow?"

"What made this happen?" said Si. "Why now?"

For a while she was quiet as if trying to sort it all out. Then she said, "Because you became a big shot. I like big shots!" And she laughed.

"No, seriously. Why did you let this happen?"

"Well, it was a romantic day on the boat, even though I made light of it. I had a great time. Then there was your job, and that seemed to call for a celebration. And my love for you—it's been simmering for a long time. I hardly admitted it to myself. But then the kettle just seemed to boil over. And as we kissed and kissed, I realized what I'd always missed in my marriage. I just couldn't control myself. And you know what? I'm glad I couldn't. But what a naughty boy you were not to control yourself!" she said playfully. Then she lifted her head off his arm and looked down at him, no longer playfully, but with adoring eyes radiating from some sacred place deep in her soul.

Then she lay again beside him and within minutes drifted off to sleep. But he lay sleepless for hours, just savoring the experience, full of love and excitement, with Saira purring in his arms.

Six weeks later Saira discovered she was pregnant.

# Chapter 13

When the new century rolled around, the Caliphate, with only a 16 percent approval rating from America's Muslims after seventy years of go-for-broke, indiscriminate mayhem, embarked on a new approach. They would continue to use violence, but direct it at the country's infrastructure rather than citizens. They would target the institutions and property of the rich and privileged, not of the common citizen, Muslim or non-Muslim. The entertainment industry turned them almost feral. As the Caliphate saw it, the grungy "music of despair" that appealed to so many young people and the "casual pornography" that poisoned so many Hollywood films should be struck down. In this way they hoped to attract the masses of decent people to their cause, which remained the same: to replace the amoral U.S. Constitution with a God-approved law, a universal sharia applicable to all citizens—Muslim, infidel, and apostate.

They began planting their bombs not in churches, schools, theaters, small businesses, and public transportation, but in large investment firms, multinational banks and insurance companies, big-time law firms, entertainment industry nerve centers, sports conglomerates that priced their tickets beyond what the common person could pay, the headquarters of legislators who feathered their nests at the expense of the ordinary taxpayer, and even the lobbies of doctors' offices off-hours who broke the backs of the middle class and poor. They tried to sell themselves to the public as "family friendly" and "tough on crime."

In professional attire—black pants and white sweater brightened by a black and orange scarf—Cindy Downham described the plan to her seven accomplices, all men. All wore the distinctive uniform of the Caliphate when they met in secret: black jeans with a gray shirt or pullover. They met in the garage of one of the men, young and single and an expert in munitions, on the outskirts of Boulder, Colorado.

"Let's go over this one more time," she said. "Our target is the cryonics institute, six miles east of here. The place houses 97 bodies and 123 brains. They're all frozen and awaiting the moment when science can give them a second life. I know this place inside and out because that's where I worked until six months ago. As you know, Brussels told us to cut back on killing. As you might not know, this place caters to rich people who think they can buy immortality. It costs $1.14 million to be a member. It's a for-profit company. The whole concept is absurd and revolting to every Muslim worthy of the name. We're going after it. Do each of you understand what you're responsible for?"

"I have a basic question before we get into that," said a clean-shaven man with the shadow of a tattoo on his neck that he'd tried to remove when he converted to Islam. "I still don't see the point. We're not killing people. We're killing mummies. What kind of a statement is that? Is that going to bring us recruits?"

The oldest man in the group spoke up. He was from headquarters in Brussels and spoke with a mild French accent. "Rodrigo, our belief is that it will. Try to see the beauty of this operation. It has all the appearance of killing, but it's not killing. The average American will see this as an exercise in restraint. By showing compassion we gain respectability, and that's something we don't have enough of. We also get the whole world's attention. Who ever heard of blowing up a cryonics asylum? As for killing, why do you want to kill? Why do any of you want to kill?"

One of the other guys, whose neatly trimmed goatee and haircut gave him a look of good breeding, spoke up. "I think this is really cool. It gives us a chance to get across our beliefs. The Caliphate will be interviewed, and they'll say that only fools think we're machines without souls. They'll say that freezing bodies defrauds people and that after 140 years of doing this shit no one has ever woken. It gives us a chance to remind people, not just Muslims, that they are souls, and souls don't need to be frozen. It's ridiculous. It's even hilarious."

"Well said, Salim," said Cindy. "It is ridiculous. But this operation has another face. And that face is *real* death. If everything goes exactly as planned, we're still going to need seven minutes. You'll be lucky to get away before the police arrive. I know there are alarms but I can't guarantee I know how they are set. Not anymore. Each of you needs to decide whether to risk a long prison term or martyr yourself. Not only that. It would be less time-consuming if one of you was in the room with all those bodies and brains. You could blow the hell out of the place, no doubt about it, and bodies and brains would be flying around like spaghetti in a tornado. I wish I could see it. Besides, it would be more certain if you detonated from the actual site. Do any of you feel in a heroic mood?"

There was quiet. No one volunteered. Then Rodrigo again spoke. "I just can't see giving up my life when they don't give up theirs. Not even one of theirs. That's crap!"

Cindy looked to the man from Brussels.

"What are you, Rodrigo, a murderer or a Muslim?" said the French accent. "We don't kill unless we have to. And now we don't have to. Do you still not understand?"

"I get it, but it just doesn't seem right."

"Rodrigo," said Cindy, "the man who martyrs himself tomorrow will have done more good for Islam than the last hundred martyrs who took a thousand lives."

Cindy studied her men and again asked, "Are any of you ready to go to Paradise?" No one volunteered. "Come on, Muslims, where is your faith?"

"Okay, I'll do it." It was Rodrigo who spoke.

Cindy's warning was flawless. All the men except the Frenchman, who was on a plane headed home to Brussels when the bomb went off, were caught. But the aluminum cylinders inside the bay where the bodies and brains were preserved were obliterated—"with a 100% fatality rate," as CNN put it. And Rodrigo went ahead to meet his fate.

Three days later Silas got a call on his personal phone from a man claiming to be a high-ranking official at Caliphate headquarters in Brussels. "I was in on the planning at Boulder," he said. He spoke perfect English but with a heavy French accent. "I regularly read your columns on religion. I see you as a journalist who tries to be fair to both sides. That is rare. I am reaching out to you for an interview. I strongly support the new policies of the Caliphate. Would you—?"

"Excuse me, but what is your name?"

"Antoine Bishara."

"Mr. Bishara, how did you find me?"

"It was a roundabout process."

"I want you to email me your full vita. And give me the number at Caliphate Central that you're calling from. It's not showing up on my phone. It's blocked."

"That's easy to do. But are you interested in the interview?"

"Yes, if you're legitimate."

Within the hour Antoine Bishara sent him the requested vita. It was impressive: Bishara took credit for masterminding many of the bombings in Europe, and a few in America.

"I can fly you to Brussels if you'd prefer," he told Silas on the second phone call.

Silas' first response was, *Not a chance—this guy is a monster, a murderer on a massive scale—I could be in danger.* But on second thought he accepted.

"You've got balls," said Stan when Si asked for the assignment. "What are you planning to do?"

"I plan on listening."

It was a raw March morning in the year 2100. Tiny snowflakes fluttered down to the cobblestone pavement in front of the refurbished Palace of Justice when Silas mounted the low steps leading between pilasters into the vast interior.

Antoine turned out to be a lawyer who did work for the Center as a volunteer. He was formally dressed in a gray coat and black tie. His icy blue eyes were Nordic.

They shook hands and traded information about flights to Belgium. "Not so easy to get here from America, I discovered," he said.

"No, we're not exactly friendly, are we?" It was hard to say whether Silas disliked Antoine on sight or because his view of the man was already corrupted. He feigned cordiality.

"No, and I wish it was otherwise," said Antoine.

A secretary dressed in a charcoal-colored borqa brought in coffee on a tray with sugar and cream on the side. Silas noted that Antoine didn't thank or even seem to notice her. The woman never looked up. Head bent down, she noiselessly drifted out like a specter.

They sat for a moment and prepared their coffee.

"I am grateful to you for coming here," Antoine said at last as he stirred in the sugar. "Tell me, were you warned that I might be dangerous?" Antoine smiled sardonically.

"Not exactly. But I was congratulated for my courage." Silas returned a rather quizzical smile.

Antoine chuckled knowingly. "Well, in any case, I am very grateful. I want to discuss our new policy of non-killing. It's almost Gandhian. I would be happy to see you endorse the policy in one of your columns."

"Ah, well, I have a lot of listening to do. Tell me about it. Why do you call it Gandhian? I am certain that some would see that as a tall claim. Many, I am quite certain, would see it as Machiavellian."

"Not at all. We are genuinely concerned not to kill unless necessary. Killing is always a last resort. What happened in Detroit was unnecessary."

"I am recording this…I take it you don't mind."

"Not at all. I value precise quoting. And I absolutely trust you to get it right. You are the best there is."

Silas saw this last comment as flattery. He was not about to be bought off, but he couldn't help disliking the man a little less. "So you are the man who contrived the Boulder bombing. That is what your vita says. No one can fault you for lack of imagination."

"That's what I'm good at: conceiving the inconceivable!"

"I happen to agree with you that death is not the end of us, but—"

"That's another reason I read you," he interrupted enthusiastically.

"—but in our country what you did was a crime."

"Not in our country," he countered.

"Well, in America people who believe death is the end have a right to hold that opinion without danger to their person—or their property. The owners of that facility weren't hurting anyone. On the contrary, they were providing a service. Not for people like us, but for people like them. At least that's how your critics would see it."

"But they were misleading people, holding out false hope, and charging for it. That's hurting people."

"Only in your opinion, your critics would say."

"No, sir, in God's opinion."

Silas wondered how in the world he could get around this kind of thinking. If he couldn't see a way, the interview might as well end. Stumped and checkmated, he stared down at his coffee cup and jiggled it. Then—

"Suppose someone were to argue in the following way: In those great cities rising out of the desert—Dubai and Doha, for example—billions are spent on buildings that have no other purpose than to show off the builder's wealth. No Muslim complains, even though it's all folly. Think of freezing bodies as one more example of human folly, and at one thousandth the cost of those buildings. Blowing up that cryonics center but not any of those buildings shows a bias. Allah tolerates human folly. Maybe he even laughs at it. It doesn't hurt anybody."

"But it does. Freezing all those bodies implies a rejection of Quranic teaching about the pleasures of Paradise."

"But doesn't wasting all that money on those buildings imply a rejection of one of the five pillars of your faith, *zakāt*, charity, almsgiving? Imagine the good that all that money could do for the poor. Allah knows that better than we do, but he puts up with gross human selfishness anyway. If Allah puts up with it, who are you not to? That's the way your critics would argue. How would you defend yourself?"

"Are you sure you're not a lawyer?" Antoine was visibly annoyed. "Look, we didn't kill anybody in Boulder. We've even placed a moratorium on beheadings. Can your critics give us a little credit!"

Silas took a deep breath to calm himself and again to collect his thoughts. "A little," he acceded, "but the abandonment of the greater evil doesn't excuse the lesser. And the destruction of private property is a lesser evil. What happened at Boulder was condemned by American Muslims not connected to your Caliphate, even though they, like you, believe in Paradise. You make it hard for them by your actions. Do you not see this?"

Antoine fidgeted. His mouth moved as if in speech, as if he were chafing at a bit, but nothing came out. Finally, he said, "Islam has more than its share of cowards."

"Let's get back to Gandhi for a moment. Back in graduate school when I was studying Hinduism, I read a lot of Gandhi. And I revered him. Apparently you appreciate him too. But Gandhi was no friend of sabotage. He condemned every kind of violence. And that included violence against property. For him terrorism degraded not only the victim but the perpetrator. It was the tactic of someone who had no patience. And that's the way your critics, especially your Muslim critics, see the Caliphate. You might want what's good in the long run—and in fact you often do—but in your haste you resort to violence. And all you end up doing is alienating the whole world and making it devilishly hard on rank-and-file Muslims who are willing to be patient. Antoine"—now Silas was willing to risk it all—"can you honestly claim that your new policy is Gandhian? Can you in all seriousness claim that Allah blesses terrorism?"

Antoine looked out of the window at the gray day. His expression was pained. Finally, he turned to Silas and said, "I think we've gone as far as we can go."

Back in New York Silas set to work on his next column. He was secretly proud to tell the world that he had infiltrated—though he did not use that word—Caliphate headquarters and interviewed the mastermind behind the Boulder bombing. It was easily the biggest coup of his budding career. The last paragraph read:

As many of my readers will hopefully grant, I have made a point of balanced reporting on the Islam question. In the process I have outraged critics who think I have been too friendly to Islam. To that I can say only, as I have said before, that there are two Islams in America. The saboteur I interviewed in Brussels last week—the very man who masterminded the Boulder bombing—reflects one of them. But the great majority of peace-loving Muslims in our country reflect the other. May they rise up, as African Americans did under the leadership of Martin Luther King, and Indians under the leadership of Mahatma Gandhi, and overthrow these impostors. But who will they rise up under? That is the great question of our time. Until it is answered, we are likely to go on as we have for another hundred years. Let us hope that this new century, the 22nd, will turn up the leader who will bring peace to our exhausted, bloodied world.

At the Friday meeting of columnists and editors, Silas's column, especially the last paragraph, came in for criticism. It ranged from its being too long to its being "too pastoral, as if written by a priest." Several agreed the tone of the piece placed too much emphasis on the part played by Silas himself, as if he were some kind of "budding prophet." But no one could argue with the thousands of replies to the column. Judging by that, it was read by over four million. And ordinary Muslims, not just spokesmen for Muslim groups, wrote in by the hundreds. Several even claimed they were the new messiah, or knew somebody who was.

Five days later Britain's newspaper *The Telegraph* reported that a fatwa of 2.3 million pounds had been raised against Silas's life. Brussels claimed he had "discredited the benevolent new policy of non-killing adopted by the Caliphate on New Year's Day 2100." No one at the Caliphate was quoted as seeing the irony of the death sentence.

# Chapter 14

Silas continued living in his NYU apartment on the understanding he would have a year to make up his mind whether to stay at NYU or resign. In his mind, he knew what he would do. The only question was whether the *Times* would be happy with his work. When it became clear after his Brussels coup that they were, he began a rather casual search for a new apartment—he still had three months on his NYU lease. He quickened his pace, however, following the fatwa. And a graffiti attack on one of the windows of the *Times* building—it read "Death to the Infidel Hypocrite, Silas Wyatt"—impelled him into action. He found a new apartment a block from the Hudson River behind Riverside Church and moved out his rather sparse furnishings within a week. He hoped the move would leave him, at least temporarily, untraceable. In any case, there was better security in his new apartment.

But Silas had other worries to deal with. Saira was due any day now, and he didn't know what to do either with her or the baby. He had proposed marriage, but she knew that would render her an apostate, even in the gentler form of Islam she loved, and she held back. Added to that, Silas wanted the baby baptized as a Christian.

There was nothing either Christian or Muslim about the birth. Silas coached her through the birth using the Lamaze technique, and the baby girl came into the world as an unaffiliated human being. They split the naming: he chose an old family name, Isabella, while she chose Inaya, which in Urdu means *concern* or *solicitude*. Her choice captured the fear of an uncertain unknown that she felt closing in on her.

Her Muslim university had rules very different from non-Muslim colleges and universities. Maternity leave did not exist for a woman giving birth outside marriage, and the father being a Christian didn't help. Saira resigned her position.

Silas was certain he could get her a job at the *Times*, but her presence there would be an embarrassment verging on the unethical. For him it approached the kind of nepotistic deal-making that he had seen at NYU and despised—so much so that he thought of trying to cover it up. Anyway, he wangled her a job as an assistant to the copy editor—the head copy editor being a machine that was just short of infallible.

A month after the birth they came to an agreement that they would give each other's religion a try "for the baby's sake." It was inconceivable to Silas that he would convert to Islam, and it was equally inconceivable to Saira that she would convert to Christianity. But neither knew with certainty how the other felt.

Walking along Fifth Avenue on a bright Sunday morning in May, Silas and Saira, with Izzy strapped on her back, shared their feelings about what they'd just witnessed: the choir Mass at St. Patrick's.

"It was beautiful," said Saira, "the incredible music, the solemn prayers, the gestures of the priests, the altar, the building itself, but it struck me as artificial. And the women in their dresses. It looked like they were going to a party. And some of them were downright sexy. All in all, it was strange. It was like you Christians are trying to create Paradise on earth."

Silas chuckled. "Well, I guess we are. What's wrong with that? I see that as a plus."

"And the sermon was hard to take. So much emphasis on Jesus. I know you Christians believe he's God, but if you step outside the indoctrination you've received since you were a boy, you'd see how, well, weird it is."

"Anything else?"

"All that kneeling and standing and sitting. But no bowing. I think the right posture in God's presence should be deep bowing, right down to the floor."

"Like at a mosque?"

"Well, yes. Why don't you Christians bow?"

"Hindus and Buddhists don't even kneel. They sit. But are they less reverent?"

"And the men and women sitting side by side. Actually I like that, but it did seem strange."

"Strange sitting next to me?"

"Yes! Especially when your hand crawled up my leg!"

Silas chuckled again. "If God were sitting next to you, he might be tempted too."

"Yeah, right! I forgot to ask you. When you were at the mosque, did you bow with the faithful, or did you sit in a chair at the back and just watch?"

"I bowed."

"You mean you got in line with all those Muslims and bowed to the floor when they did?"

"I did."

"That's hilarious! I would have paid to see that! How did it feel?"

"Frankly, it felt rather ridiculous. I felt like I was groveling to keep on the good side of an emperor sitting on a throne out in the cosmos somewhere."

"Silas, you are so wrong. This is not about groveling, but about the finite meeting the infinite. It's natural to bow. It feels good to bow. Besides, all that bodily movement keeps the mind focused. If you just sit still, your mind wanders."

"Hmm, you've got a point there. Still, sons don't bow to their father, and most Christians think of God as their father. How would you feel if your sons and daughters bowed down to the floor in front of you? If I were God, I would forbid it. In my version of the Quran it would be forbidden: *haram!*"

"It's a good thing you're not God, Si, or the sun would rise in the west and set in the east, like it's supposed to when the world comes to an end."

"When that happens, I'll be sure to convert. That's a promise."

They walked on as people streamed past them and cabs of various colors dodged each other to let their customers in or out. Silas said, "Did I ever tell you my great-grandfather used to drive one of these to earn a little cash? It got him through school back in the twenties?"

"Really?" She seemed to be distracted, not listening.

He tried again. "Have you ever noticed how everybody who walks past us looks at you and not me?"

"Oh, that's because they want to see what's in the papoose."

"No, no. It happens in restaurants too. Waitresses always look at you first. Why do you suppose that is?"

"I never noticed. Maybe you just look too serious."

They caught up with and passed three burqas. Silas noted how oddly cheerful, like school girls chatting, their voices sounded.

"Izzy, Izzy, Izzy, hasn't she been good!" he said, reaching over to touch her bald little head as they clopped along. "Her Majesty slept all the way through the Mass, and only now is she waking up. Ooooh, and more than waking up. Do you smell that? Here, let me get a picture of the two of you."

"A picture? Why now? Okay, but hurry. But wait a minute. Let me put on my hijab."

"Your hijab? You don't wear a hijab. What in the world —"

"It's part of the deal. The hijab is part of Islam, just like party dresses are part of Christianity. Besides, I look good in a hijab."

"You look good in anything." They stopped, and Saira pulled out a sky-blue hijab from her purse and wrapped it around her head. Then she flashed her most radiant smile as Silas aimed his phone at the perfect oval that was her face. "You know, I don't even have a picture of you in my apartment." Then he leaned over to kiss the bald head with the stinky diaper.

One of the pledges they made to each other was to read their respective scriptures for ten minutes each night. Silas had his Quran sitting on the table next to his reading chair. Also on the table was the picture he took of Saira and Izzy on Fifth Avenue, which he had put in a frame only the day before.

He was sitting at his desk working on an article contrasting the worship styles of the world's religions and what probably lay behind them. There was a knock at the door. *That's odd*, he thought. There had been no buzz from the entrance. He got up and warily approached the door, uncertain what to do. But when a pleasant voice said, "I have a package for a Silas Wyatt," he cracked open the door.

The door was violently pushed into him as the chain snapped, and he fell back on the floor. "Stay where you are!" said a man holding a pistol stretched out at him. "Say your last prayers. I'll give you a minute before I send you off to hell. Make the least move and you won't get that."

In shock, Silas tried to stay calm. On one occasion when he couldn't sleep he had actually imagined a scenario something like this. But now all he could say in a voice that quivered was, "Hey man, you've got the wrong guy."

"Oh yeah? We'll see. Show me your identification. Where is your wallet?"

Silas looked over at his desk where his wallet sat and concluded he was done for. He said a prayer: "Oh God, take me to you." He glanced at the picture of mother and baby on the stand, with mother wearing a hijab, and his prayer turned to despair.

"Show me your wallet, blasphemer," the intruder said, jabbing his weapon at his prey. He had a full black beard and a small mole above his upper lip.

"Over there," Silas said feebly, pointing at the desk.

"Don't move an inch or you get the bullet." The man walked over to the desk, never taking his eyes off Silas while turning the gun toward him as he moved.

The man glanced quickly at Silas's municipal ID card. "Silas

Wyatt, there it is. The slime who wrote that article."

"You're after the fatwa," said Silas to drag out what little time was left. "How did you find me?"

"What does it matter? Have you finished saying your prayers?"

"Prayers?" Silas hardly heard himself say the word. His mind was racing as his eyes fixed on the picture. A scenario was forming in his mind, a desperate last chance to cheat death.

"Get down on your knees and bend over," the man said. "Better not to watch."

Silas made as if to get up and bend over, but then halted. "Regarding the fatwa, I don't think you're up to date. It was cancelled."

"Cancelled? What lie is this!"

"Look, look over at the table. What do you see? That's a picture of my wife and baby. My wife in the hijab. They're visiting my mother. And what is that book you see? Go and look at it."

Still pointing the pistol at Silas, the man walked over to the table and glanced at the Quran in English translation.

Silas watched the man turn back from the table and said: "You're a Sunni Muslim, and that's what I'll be if you don't kill me first. My wife converted me. That woman over there, with the hijab. Yes, I am Silas Wyatt, the writer of that article. The ex-columnist for the *Times*. That man is already dead. The man you see now—he's about to convert. That woman you see, that mother of my daughter—she brought me to repentance. I will publicly repudiate that heretical tract in front of the whole world. The Caliphate will make a big deal out of it. There will be a ceremony, a conversion ceremony. In Brussels. I've been invited to Brussels for the ceremony. The word just came out. I guess you haven't heard. Then I'll work for the Caliphate. I'll make up for my stupid mistake in a thousand ways. If you kill me, you'll send a martyr to Paradise. And hell will be your fate. They issued a fatwa on anyone who kills me. They have great plans for me. And you'll deny that little girl" —he pointed to the picture— "a father."

The man looked bewildered, and his arm drooped.

"As-salaamu-alaikum, Brother," Silas said as he got off the floor and stretched out his arms in greeting.

The man looked at Silas in utter confusion, then answered, "Wa-alaikumu-as-salaam." He stuck his pistol in his coat pocket and took Silas's hand.

"My new name is Kabir, and who are you?"

"I am Nadheer, just a humble Yemeni stock boy at a neighborhood grocery store. I have a wife and son. Please forgive me. I did not know."

"You're a good man, Nadheer, and I will tell the Caliphate about your bravery. And tell your wife that my wife sends her warm greetings. Perhaps someday we will meet again. Perhaps in Paradise."

Silas kissed both Nadheer's cheeks and led him to the door. Both men offered both their hands in a compact clasp. They parted like blood kin.

As soon as the door was closed and locked, Silas called 911. Six minutes later the police called him back and asked him to come down to the station to identify the man. It was Nadheer.

Dostoevsky was required reading for Silas, nineteen at the time, in a class at the University of Wisconsin in existentialist philosophy. His professor told the class that in 1849 Dostoevsky as a young man had been condemned to death by a firing squad for sedition against the tsar. The professor showed the class a drawing of the scene: three young men blindfolded and tied to pillars, with twenty rifles aimed at them, and graves dug at their feet. Dostoevsky knew he would be in the next threesome, and a fearful despair enveloped him. But at the last instant a "reprieve" was announced. The whole scene had been staged to teach the young rebels a lesson. Silas didn't have to spend the next four years in Siberia like Dostoevsky, but the lesson he learned from Nadheer was the same. With all his might he wanted to live. Not even his research into the afterlife took away that primal urge. That night he fell on his knees and prayed, prayed with a fervor he had never known before, to a God he knew he did not understand and could not define.

# Chapter 15

Izzy was now five. Saira had resisted marriage time and again, and Silas suspected she was holding out for a liberal Muslim man whose scruples regarding marriage to a Muslim woman with a bastard child she could overcome with her beauty. In the meantime she refused to allow sex to get out of hand as it did when Izzy was conceived. She managed to think of herself as a "renewed virgin," she once quipped. His frustrated desire for her almost maddened him, and arguments followed. He warned her he would begin looking elsewhere for a wife. He computer-dated, and he had no trouble finding Christians "between thirty and forty, with or without a child." But at best they provided good company. They never measured up to Saira. He was forty, hugely successful, and lonely, with no one to go home to at the end of the day.

Saira and Layla kept in touch, mostly by texting, and that is how he learned that Layla, who had a four-year-old daughter of her own, had been divorced by her husband a few months before. Saira didn't know the details, but she said the breakup was amicable and more or less mutual. When Silas heard of this development, his imagination ran wild. Marriage to Layla, his first sweetheart and the most noble—that was exactly the right word—the most noble woman he had ever met, would be no mere consolation prize. He was tempted to call her immediately, but thought better of it and decided to wait a few weeks.

A few days later a surprise arrived in the mail at his office. His secretary, with a grin, delivered it to him on a tray. "From your great-great-grandmother," she joked. It was a physical letter with the address written out in longhand and a stamp on it. He handled it as if it were an archaeological find. He knew right away it was from Layla. He opened the letter and began to read.

Dear Silas,

As you have no doubt heard from Saira, I have been divorced by my husband. I find myself harking back to our last time together. Do you remember the Moroccan restaurant? Do you remember how I recommended you seek out Saira and befriend her so you could take your mind off me? I have regretted those words.

I hardly know why I've chosen to write you in this old-fashioned way. I remember how you loved my handwriting. Do you remember your joke about my being a Chinese calligrapher in a previous life? More likely it's because the loops and whorls of my script better express what is in my heart. Let me try to come straight to the point. I gave too much weight to the laws and edicts and codes that I thought defined a good Muslim woman, and too little to my own nature and the love I felt for you. It surprises me to hear that you are still unmarried, and I wonder if those feelings you had for me then are alive now. I know that you and Saira are close friends and were once lovers. I would not be writing this if you and she still were. Forgive me if I have misjudged that relationship; I would never permit myself to come between the two of you. But something is holding you back from marrying her—or is it the other way round? In any case, if you are the same man I knew and once loved so well, there would be nothing to hold *me* back. Can you believe I am speaking so bluntly? It frightens me to imagine how you might be pitying me if my love for you is not returned. But as they say, nothing ventured, nothing gained.

Please don't see this as a clumsy proposal. See it as a crying out for the renewal of something wonderful. The longer I lived with Rajeed—he's a physician—the more I found myself thinking of you. Oh, how I fought it! He is a good man and a good father to my little daughter, but he could tell that I was, as they say, going through the motions; and I think my cooling induced a cooling in him. Well, he found another woman, a nurse with whom he worked closely, and gave me the option of staying on or leaving. Without hesitation I chose to leave. I am sure he and his fiancée were relieved. And so was I when he, with his sixty-hour work schedule, granted me custody over little Safiya. I don't mean to say that I wasn't hurt. But I was also thrilled because I was free. My university has loosened up on the mixed marriage issue since Saira left, and I'm almost certain they would do no more than frown at my marrying a Christian. I am ready to do that if you will have me.

So there you are. If you are not interested, I will survive. My work is meaningful, and invitations to speak keep coming my way, some with surprisingly impressive honorariums. My heart will ache, but it will not break. I am a stranger to depression.

I look forward to hearing from you, but please, only by post or email. I couldn't bear hearing your voice just before you gave the verdict, and I might go to pieces for a little while if the answer were no.

Your loving Layla

When Silas finished reading the letter he was shivering. He was moved to ecstasy at the thought of marriage to Layla, but that ecstasy was tinged with misgiving at the thought of its impact on Saira. What would Saira say? How could they continue working in the same building? How could he bear to see her unhappy? Or would she take it nonchalantly? Was she less in love with him than he thought? And there was Izzy to consider. Marrying Layla would mean seeing less of his daughter. And the relation between Saira and Layla, at one time so prized by both, would be fraught. But the thought of being united with his first and greatest love intoxicated him. But was she still his greatest love? He had thought of her for such a long time as completely out of reach that he wasn't sure. For years Saira had replaced her. He never dreamed he would be forced to make a choice. But one thing was certain: Marriage to either was immensely better than no marriage at all. Coming home to a loving wife and bringing a child or two into the world was a major goal of his life, almost the only one yet to be realized. Though he shuddered at the thought of Saira suffering, he saw no alternative. But the more he thought about it, the more he realized he would suffer too. He would miss her passion, her sense of humor, her sassiness, her mind, her beauty. The thought of Saira out of his life frightened him. How could he tell her? He dreaded the moment. But there was no denying what he had to do.

They met in her apartment during Izzy's nap time three days after he read the letter. Paintings and tapestries hung from the walls of her cozy one-room apartment not far from the 9/11 Memorial and Museum—an apartment made affordable by his hefty child support payments. There were no pictures of human beings. He noticed on the wall a qibla compass that Saira used to point herself in the direction of Mecca when she prayed. There were flourishing leafy plants in colorful clay pots along the wall next to the window looking down over the street below. She wore silky white harem pants adorned with green and gold butterflies. Her long black hair fell freely over her shoulders.

She brought out two cups of tea in porcelain cups with intricate blue etchings and stirred in honey and lemon in his case, cream in hers.

They sat facing each other with a low wooden table between them and sipped their tea.

"You look very mysterious this afternoon," Saira said. "You have one of those intimidating scowls I've warned you about, my love. Is something troubling you?"

"Well, something surprising has come up. How often do you hear from Layla?"

"Layla. Maybe once every two weeks. We text each other,

though three months ago we had a short talk on the phone about her divorce. Why? Is she all right? I didn't think you were in contact with her."

"No, I hadn't been. I hadn't heard from her since her marriage, more than five years ago. But I got a letter from her Wednesday. She wrote it in longhand. It came to my office at the *Times*. She said—hang on to your seat—that she was open to marrying me. No, that she *wanted* to marry me."

Now it was Saira's turn to scowl. Silas couldn't help noticing that she splashed a little tea on her lovely pants. "Damn!" she said. And she rushed to the kitchen to wipe off the spill.

"Are you okay?" said Silas.

She came back in a fluster. "Not really. What are you going to do?"

"You know how I love you, Saira. You are the mother of our child, and we have been through a lot together. I respect and profoundly admire you. I've watched you reach out to women's groups all over the city. You're a force for all I see as good and necessary on the Islam question. You and I are almost like partners in some ways. But—"

"Yes?"

"You won't marry me. And Layla will. And I love Layla too. You're as different as, well, these porcelain cups from those flower pots over by the window, but I love you both. Deeply and profoundly love you both. But I can marry only one of you. And I intend to marry. You know that. I've wanted it for a long time."

"So you will be marrying Layla because I won't marry you— is that what you're saying?"

"I'm afraid so."

"And there is no other reason?"

"If there is, I haven't found it yet. No, there's no other reason, at least none that weighs as heavily."

"Silas, what would you do if I agreed to marry you? That's what I'd like to know."

"Well, just off the top of my head, I would be inclined to say I'd marry you. We have a child together, and—"

"Suppose we didn't. What then? That's what I'd like to know. No child. Now, please, go to work. Think it through. Carefully."

Silas leaned back against his chair and looked up at the ceiling. For a minute he said nothing, just stared. "I don't know, Saira. I really don't. You are just so different. Each lovely in such different ways. So why not let Izzy be the deciding factor?"

"Would you give up seeing Izzy if you chose Layla? Why should Izzy matter? You could see her every day if you wanted to."

"Frankly, I'd prefer living with my own child over living with someone else's."

"So I'm just thrown in with the bargain so you can live with Izzy."

"Oh, come on, Saira! That's not what I'm saying at all. I'm just saying Izzy is the…is the tie-breaker."

"The tie-breaker!? Silas, I want you to go home and search your heart. Who do you want to spend the rest of your days with? Who do you love more? Forget about Izzy. And remember, if you choose me, there will be all the love-making you could ever want."

"Let me be clear about this. You're now saying you'll marry me—after all these months of saying you wouldn't. Why? Why the change of heart?"

"You know why. You're forcing my hand. I…I love you and I—" Suddenly her eyes watered, and she brought her hand in a fist to her forehead, and stammered, "and I couldn't bear losing you! I just wish you were a Muslim!"

Silas was struck dumb. He had wanted to hear these words for a long time, ever since the magical day on Ethan's boat, and now that they had come he didn't know what to do. His first inclination was to pick her up and carry her into the bedroom, but he thought of Layla.

He finally said, "I love you too, darling Saira, don't ever doubt that."

She wiped her eyes and looked up at him. "You can't tell me now which it is?"

He sighed and said, "I need time. I need to go home and think—even pray."

"Don't forget about Izzy, Si!"

"Izzy? I thought you said—"

"Oh, I am so confused! Forgive me. That was stupid. That wasn't fair."

He got up, leaned over, and kissed her wet cheek.

"Before you go," she said, "tell me one thing: am I the flower pot or the porcelain cup?"

He was amazed at the question and had no idea how to answer. Finally he said, "You're neither. I was just setting up a contrast. It was a weak metaphor. A stupid metaphor. You're just different. That's all. I need to go home and sort it out. Just remember: however it turns out, my love for you will never waver."

The next day Silas sat in front of his computer at home and tried to work on an article on the fatwas that twenty-four American citizens were living under. He was one of them. Were the threats empty, meant only to terrify? Most of them, probably. But not all. There had been twenty-six the previous year. But the two victims of the twenty-six had directly insulted the Prophet, and he hadn't done that. Thank God! Anyway, he knew what it was like to look behind his back when he walked the streets of New York: two months ago someone had upped the reward for his head, this time in dollars. So he had a lot to say about fatwas, the terror they bred, and how to handle that terror and get along with a normal life. For the first time he was going public with his own encounter with death. He dared to tell the story because he had twice visited Nadheer in prison and even sent a little money to Nadheer's wife—the simple man still had twelve years to go—and he felt that mention of this would take the hounds off his track. But he couldn't work further on the article no matter how hard he tried, even with a strict self-imposed deadline.

*To hell with it,* he told himself. He clicked on a "favorite" on his computer that he hadn't used for a longtime, the one that read *Layla.* He would honor her wish for a message delivered by post, printed out on paper. He took a deep, anxious breath and began.

My beloved Layla,

For the last twenty-two hours I've been sorting out my feelings about your proposal. I've never agonized over something so much. Jesus is said to have sweat blood the day before he died—such was his suffering—and I can almost relate to that. What I am about to say is almost unbearable. No one of your nature and character should ever have to experience this.

I have decided to marry Saira, but not because I prefer her. Trying to discover a preference has led me around in endless circles. The decision is strictly rational. Izzy is my child, and I want to be with her as she grows up—that's the main consideration. In the final analysis, it's the only one. It relieves me to know that your little Safiya is supported by her father and that your life is full and professionally rewarding, but that is only a secondary factor, though one I am very grateful for.

You cannot imagine how it breaks my heart to tell you this. My love for you is profound; there is something about it that feels eternal, as eternal as the soul that makes me the unique being I am. I cannot imagine not knowing and loving you on the other side of what we call death. As for now, I can only hope that your knowledge of this love will bring you solace and even joy.

Do not for a moment think that you are weeping alone. My eyes are filled with tears as I type. That this letter has to end in this way—or at all—is heartbreaking. But be assured: this is not the end of a relationship. When you think of me, do not doubt that a day will ever pass without my thinking of you.

Tearfully and with a heart bursting with love,

Si

Silas had worked hard on a short paragraph he didn't send. It read:

It is entirely possible that in the end we will be united after all. Saira is an intrepid risk-taker, and her language is colorful and designed to incite. At heart she is a revolutionary. As she becomes better known and draws a bigger stage, she is likely to earn a fatwa, like me. God forbid that anything should happen to her, but...

Ever since he was a teenager, his father had told him he had a tendency to say too much, especially if it was the truth. On looking back to the fiasco at NYU with his colleagues, he wondered if that had been the problem. Of course it was possible that Saira could be gunned down by the Caliphate, but did one need to say it? Especially as a way of holding out hope for a happy reunion with another? It was possible. But did one need to say it? *For God's sake, save me from myself!* he exclaimed to himself. And he deleted the passage.

# Chapter 16

Between 2106 and 2108 the Great Influenza pandemic wiped out 9 percent of the world's population. Especially hard hit were India, Pakistan, Bangladesh, and Sri Lanka, which collectively lost an unthinkable 21 percent of their people, with Bangladesh at 32 percent. South Asia became one vast charnel ground. In India there wasn't enough timber to accommodate all the Hindu deaths in its northern cities; individual cremation gave way to mass burial. Where population was relatively thin, as in the United States, the rate of mortality was much reduced, with only 2 percent of Americans struck down. Many fundamentalists of various faiths said the plague was caused by being a member of the wrong religion.

Silas's old friend Ethan Drayton, still unretired and working his customary magic making money for the super-rich, was scheduled to give the keynote address for an international group of financiers meeting in Kyoto, Japan, in April 2109. The financial markets were just starting to squeak back out of the historic beating they took, and Ethan, who had adroitly sniffed out the right moment for shorting the markets three years before, was now expected to make the call in the opposite direction. The smart money knew a reversal, and possibly a boom, was coming; the only question was when. Ethan was the man who was supposed to tell them.

Ethan didn't want to travel alone and wondered if he could coax Silas into coming with him.

"Hey, hotshot, how would you like to see Japan next month?" Ethan said over the phone. "It'll be cherry blossom season, and I've got to go there to give a talk and advise my vassals. Can you get free?"

"Well—"

"You know they're just about the only country in the world

the Caliphate hasn't infiltrated. You can walk around without looking over your shoulder, pal. And I've got a surprise for you—an interview with Toshihiro Shima."

"What? The Prime Minister? Are you kidding?"

"I can't guarantee it, but I'm pretty sure. I've set aside time, just him and me. I've been his financial adviser for the last twenty-five years—before he became famous. I've made him a fortune. I'm even staying in his home a couple of nights."

"Jesus, Ethan! You've got to be kidding. I knew you had pull, but this! How long will you be there?"

"Five days and six nights. Two weeks away. I'll cover your expenses if the *Times* won't. What do you say?"

"Are you kidding? Do you think I'd pass *that* up? I'll work it out with Saira."

"You do that. And bring your hiking boots. They tell me there are some great pilgrimage trails in the mountains south of Kyoto. With your background, you can't afford to miss that."

Hiking pilgrimage trails—an interview with the great man who united the two Koreas—insight into Japan's blockade of the Caliphate: Silas saw three or four columns jumping out at him at once, maybe four or five. And all in five days. That was the kind of efficiency he liked.

Ethan bought two round-trip non-stop tickets between New York and Osaka. The *Times* was happy to pick up the tab.

Japan's celebrated elderly sage and leader, now eighty; Wall Street's world-class financier, now seventy-three; and Silas, the forty-four-year-old pup, sat on high cushions on three sides of a square table in the middle of a spacious room looking out at a garden with a pink-blossomed cherry tree its centerpiece. Tatami mats, alternating between chestnut and beige, covered the floor in well-defined segments. In one of the corners stood a bonsai, and on the wall facing Silas a picture of a mist-filled mountain scene hung, reminding him of the rainy day he had spent in the mountains the day before. A lamp came down from the ceiling directly over the table. This was the home of Toshihiro Shima, Nobel Peace Prize winner and the leader of Japan's Liberal Democratic Party. It was heady stuff even for a *Times* columnist. Silas approached the great man with awe.

An exquisite elderly lady dressed in a kimono and carrying teacups bowed her way in and out of the room.

"Ah, Mr. Wyatt, did you enjoy your hike?" began the sage in accented but easily understandable English.

"Very much, sir. Especially yesterday, the day it rained. I prefer nature in motion to nature at rest."

"Ah!" the old man laughed, "so you got wet!" His wrinkled old face beamed with mirth.

"I did. But it didn't prevent me from stopping at the shrines and saying a prayer."

Mr. Shima seemed pleased. "What is your impression of Japan so far? Our friend here tells me you are a reporter for the *New York Times* and were once a professor. That is quite a responsibility. What will you tell the world about us in your next column?"

"Sir, what I feel after so short an introduction is that—I hope this doesn't come across as too dramatic—is that Japan is the world's only First World country."

"Ah! Now that is a surprise. Please, tell me what you mean."

"Well, please understand that I am going by first impressions. But there is no denying what I've seen. There is no litter anywhere, not in your cities, not along the trails. Not one plastic bottle. There is no graffiti staining your buildings. Your trains run smoothly and noiselessly—I've never heard a horn or a whistle. And they run on time to the minute. So do your buses. There are no potholes on your roads. Your buildings are clean and handsome. I'm yet to see a slum. All of this is amazing. It makes America seem trashy and backward by comparison—though I won't put it so bluntly in my column. And there is almost no violent crime, maybe because nobody owns a gun. I read that there were only six gun deaths in all Japan last year. In America there were over fifty thousand. And I love the way you greet each other, with a bow, and often a smile. All of this represents to me a high civilization. And, of course, there is all the natural beauty."

"Ah! You honor us more than we deserve. There are more ways to kill than with guns, my young friend. We have a special problem with suicide. But your specialty, I understand, is religion. You said nothing about our religion."

"If I didn't know better, I'd say Japan was one of the most religious countries in the world. On the trail I came across Jizo statues everywhere. And I spent an hour at Nachi-san and watched people bow reverently as they entered sacred space under the torii and the great trees. Yet the polls say Japan is one of the least religious countries in the world. Maybe you can explain."

"Ah! It pleases me to see that you know who Jizo is and that you have seen Nachi-san. You are no ordinary tourist."

"That's true. I've studied religion. Like you, if what Ethan tells me is true, I value religion and want to see more of it, but of the right kind."

A wonderful breeze blew in from the garden through the open space between the drawn shoji screens. Mr. Shima turned to Ethan and asked if he desired more tea. "No, thank you, but do ask our young friend what he would like to do with his life."

"Ah, how surprising. I thought he was already doing much with his life." The old man turned back to Silas. "Our friend wants me to ask what you want to do with your life. So I ask you, and I hope the question is not impertinent."

"Not at all. If I could, I would like to be a politician, like you."

"Ah! And why is that?"

"Because all I do is write, whereas you control. You make things happen. Take Korea. I could only deplore the war between the two Koreas and recommend solutions. But you actually brought them together and changed the world. You made history. I just reflect on it."

"Ah, you overestimate the part I played. Once the North's leaders bombed Seoul, American bombers played a far more decisive role. Within a month everybody who was still alive was desperate for peace—on both sides. I was glad to help, but for me it was easy."

"I am sure you are too modest."

The grand old man smiled serenely at Silas and said, "So you really want to make the world a better place."

"That's always been my hope, my ambition. For you the issue was the two Koreas. For me it's something else. What else is there to do but help the world struggle along with a little less suffering?"

Mr. Shima held his peace and quietly studied Silas. Then he said, "You think big. So did I when I was your age. Today my hopes are more modest. My first ambition is to die in peace and go to the world of my ancestors beyond. But I am the country's leader, so I cannot rest yet."

Silas couldn't believe what was happening. This great man was honoring him with an intimacy he didn't expect or deserve, and Silas couldn't help loving the old man in return. He said, "I too want to die in peace and go beyond. It was this wish, as long as I can remember, that sent me to Divinity School. But now I have to live in this world and try to fix it."

"And what would you like to fix? Climate? The next virus?"

"That's important, but for me, in my own country, the Caliphate problem. The problem that doesn't exist in Japan. The problem your country has solved but is menacing the rest of the world. I was hired by the *Times* to write about this, to grapple with it, to do my little part even to defeat it. Of course, I've read a great deal about Japan's approach, but I'd be grateful, very grateful, to hear it from you."

"Noriko," he called back to his wife in Japanese, "we are going into the garden. We'll sit around the pond. Have Aki bring three chairs. And would you bring me my jacket?" Then, as he rose, he turned to Ethan and said, "Your friend" —he stole a glimpse at Silas—"is putting me to work!" And he chuckled. "But first let us go outside and listen to the birds and frogs."

They rose and stepped between the screens out into the cool air of a garden of carefully trimmed oak and maple, a single cherry tree in radiant pink-tinged bloom, rounded scarlet azaleas, a bowed bridge over a small pond with lotuses and fish flashing their orange colors, rocks and paths of white sand, and green velvety moss. They took their seat at the foot of the pond, and Toshihiro Shima began: "Did you know that my name, *shima*, means *island*? Our geography gives us a natural advantage, do you not think?"

Silas nodded.

"We fight the plague in three ways. Number one, we do not allow anyone except a few farmers and the police to own guns. You cannot buy them in stores, and there is no black market. The Japanese hate guns. They have since our defeat in the Second World War. Without guns, how can the Caliphate operate? Number two, we have a propaganda ministry that makes Facebook, despite all their efforts, look like schoolboy play. As CALIPHACE is poisoning the rest of the world with their propaganda, we are keeping pace with them, or at least coming close. We intercept the messages from their satellites with great skill and at great cost. Their messages don't get through to our people. We don't allow it. Number three, we have another ministry that keeps track of every Muslim in the country. We visit their homes and ask them questions, mostly about their children's education."

"Yes, I've read about this," said Silas. "In America we call this profiling and don't permit it."

"Ah, but our Muslims understand the need and hate the Caliphate as much as the rest of us. We train our social workers to treat them with great respect when we enter their homes on the annual visit, and they are patient with us. Very few complain, but I am aware the rest of the world does."

"I read a few years ago that if someone from a family leaves the country and joins the Caliphate, the rest of the family is deported. Has that become a problem?"

"Not at all. Every Muslim family understands the policy. It provides a powerful incentive to steer their kids in the right direction. Last year there was not a single deportation."

"How many Muslims are there in Japan?"

"About 130,000."

"Out of a hundred twenty million. That's not much more than one in a thousand."

"That is correct. We have a strict immigration policy. Not directed at Muslims, but at all outsiders. Is it true that you are married to a Muslim?"

Silas was well aware of the policy and had mixed feelings about it. He decided not to direct any more questions at his gracious host. To Mr. Shima's question he nodded a circumspect yes.

On their way back into the house, Silas asked where the bodyguards were.

"Ah! Bodyguards! Did you notice Aki? You took him to be a servant? No, he is Special Security. He even carries a gun."

As they parted and Silas began mounting the stairs to his room, the old sage looked up at him, smiled, and said, "If you want to go into politics, then go, but do not expect much. No one meddles with a writer or teacher, but every politician has to dominate a dozen other voices if he is to get anywhere. The best excuse for being a politician is to learn how to negotiate, a valuable skill."

"Thank you, sir," said Silas, bowing deeply. "I will take that to heart."

Later in the year, just before Christmas, Saira told him she had a Christmas present for him. At the age of thirty-eight, she was pregnant with an unplanned tiny son, to be born the following summer. They decided to call him Eliot Sharif.

# Chapter 17

WNYC, New York's public radio station, produced a show on religion every Sunday morning from 10:00 to 11:00. The purpose was not only to make the public more aware of the world's many religions, but above all to encourage tolerance of them by nonbelievers and harmony among people of different faiths. The station found it easy to line up speakers from every religion except Islam. The reason, it was assumed, was that Muslims who spoke out publicly for tolerance, especially if they praised other religions, were putting themselves at risk. Sometimes an audience of two hundred completely filled the studio, leaving standing room only. It was WNYC's most popular locally produced program.

Every Sunday was different. But in programs featuring a Muslim, one could depend on representatives from the Caliphate attending, and they had been known to be disruptive. On this particular sleety Sunday morning in December 2112, speakers representing six of the world's major faiths were asked to respond to the question, "If you had been born into and were devoutly practicing a religion different from the one you actually practice today, what would be your attitude toward your present religion?" The show's producers had not been able to attract a Muslim speaker, but one of the producers was a faithful reader of Silas's columns and asked him for help. Silas immediately thought of Saira. For years she had been addressing small study groups all over the metropolitan area, but she had no formal credentials, no Ph.D. in religious studies, no affiliation with a mosque, and no close relation to an imam. In a word, she had not been discovered. *Now, at last, is her chance,* thought Silas. But he was reluctant. Her views were more progressive than Connor al-Anzi's back in Detroit, and he had paid for them with his head. Silas didn't want a second fatwa in the family.

Silas aired his concerns with her. "Bear in mind, many of the enemy will be tuned in—the program is broadcast all over the country. And a few will probably be in the live audience. They'll be putting questions to you, trying to trap you. They'll try to confuse you, lead you off topic. So far you've had little dealing with people like them. Up till now your audiences have always been safe."

Saira had been sitting across from Silas at the breakfast table watching Eliot in his highchair demolish a deviled egg. She leveled a scowl at Silas and said, "Do you really think I'm not up to it? Do you think I'm no match for those misogynist ignoramuses? I'll show them what a woman can do. And I'll show *you*." He called back his contact and volunteered Saira. The show was set.

The panelists sat at a long, narrow table. In front of each was the name and the religion: Hinduism, Judaism, Buddhism, Christianity, Islam, Sikhism. The studio was a large room miked from a single invisible source at the ceiling.

The program went along in humdrum fashion. The Buddhist, Hindu, and Sikh all imagined themselves members of each other's religions as alternates, with reincarnation and eternal liberation from the wheel of rebirth a common thread. So their self-critiques went off gently—too gently for an audience hoping for a little fireworks. Even the Jew, who happened to be a Kabbalist, believed in reincarnation, so his religion did not suffer from too big a contrast. The Christian might have chosen the perspective of a Jew, but instead she boldly chose to look at her religion from the perspective of a Hindu, and in this way brought out the more obvious contrasts between the two religions.

For reasons not explained, Saira, wearing the same sky-blue hijab she wore when Silas took her picture on Fifth Avenue ten years before, was asked to speak last. She had the crowd, including Silas and ten-year-old Izzy, sitting in anxious anticipation. She began:

"I am deeply honored and excited to be here among you,

even though I have no distinction or degree compared to those of my fellow panelists. Perhaps that's why I approach the question somewhat differently. I didn't think we were being asked to distinguish our religion from other religions, but to say what we thought of it from an alien perspective. So let us suppose I had been born a Christian in Boston or a Hindu in Mumbai. What would I have thought of Islam? Can't you guess? I would have thought of it as a false religion and maybe even a threat to world peace. Was that a gasp I heard? But I am only being honest. My husband is a Christian, so I—"

"She's a fraud, a plant!" a shrill voice in the back shouted. "There is no Muslim on the program!"

"Sir," said the veteran moderator, a Greek and Coptic scholar from Fordham's Lincoln Center campus, "you'll have a chance to speak after she's finished. Any more outbursts like that from the audience, and you'll be escorted out of the building by one of the guards. And just for the record, Saira Wyatt is a Muslim, and we are lucky to have her. Ms. Wyatt, please continue."

"I was going to say that I'm lucky to be married to a Christian scholar who can sort true Islam from false Islam, and can love the one while hating the other. I've learned from him. But let me continue. Now let's imagine I'm a Hindu. I would look at the claim that there is no God but Allah and ask, 'But what about Krishna, what about Shiva, what about the Mother?' And I would look at the claim that Muhammad is the last and the greatest of the prophets and ask, 'But you've never heard of Kabir, or Mirabai, or Yogananda?' So I'd look at Islam through the eyes of a disbeliever. It would not be my religion. I would love another God as much as I love Allah. I would love another prophet or sage as much as I love Muhammad. I would regard the Bhagavad Gita as the word of God, not the Quran. And I would assume Muslims would have to undergo many rebirths before they awoke from their delusion as Allah's servants. That is how I'd look at my religion if I'd been born a Hindu in Mumbai. I hope, sir, that I've done justice to the question asked."

"You have indeed, and most eloquently," said the moderator. Now he looked out at the audience and asked for questions. Ten hands shot up. "Yes, the woman in the back. Who would you like to address your question to?"

"To Professor Mehta."

"Yes?" said the Professor.

"You are a Hindu, and you have heard your religion praised by a Muslim. What is your response?"

"Well, frankly, I was surprised, I'd almost say shocked. To put it mildly, I was impressed by her knowledge of my religion."

"I wonder if you could imagine yourself a Muslim and describe your feelings about Hinduism. In other words, do in reverse what Saira Wyatt did," said the woman.

"Actually, that would not be too hard. I would condemn all attempts to picture God and strongly object to the many gods we love. And the whole notion of many rebirths I would regard as absurd. That's just a beginning. No two religions are more unlike than Islam and Hinduism."

"So who is right?" said the woman.

"It depends who is speaking, I suppose."

"Thank you," said the moderator. "The young man in the back."

"I loved what Saira Wyatt said. But I'd like to hear more. Mrs. Wyatt, you have a pretty good grasp of Hinduism and, I assume, Christianity, since your husband is a Christian. You seem to understand that if you'd been born to a different set of parents, you'd probably have a different religion. Do I have this right?"

"Yes, you do."

"Then, what conclusions do you draw from that? I mean, suppose you *had* been born a Hindu? Would Allah condemn you to hell for worshipping several gods and believing in reincarnation and not accepting Muhammad as his prophet?"

"That's a great question, and I thank you for it. Let me back up. Over the years I've studied the major religions of the world and even taken a few courses in them. I hope I won't shock anyone by saying they are alternate paths to God. How could God, or Allah, condemn someone because he or she was born to one set of parents instead of another? That deity would be a lunatic, a sadist, not God at all. If that was the way God was, I'd prefer the deepest, darkest hell over paradise. For at least I wouldn't have to live under the eyes of such a monster. But God isn't like that. God cares less about what religion we profess than about how we live our lives. Are we forces for good or evil? That's what matters."

"I agree completely. But why, then, why be a Muslim? Why wear the hijab? Why Islam?"

"Why not? I'm familiar with it. I was raised in it. For the same reason I want my husband to come home at night rather than a stranger. I know my husband, I'm familiar with him, he makes me happy when he walks through the door. The stranger might be as good a man as my husband, or better looking, or even a Muslim! But he's not the man I'm married to. Now suppose I'd been born a Hindu, and was familiar with that religion, and loved that religion, that would be reason enough for me to be a Hindu, right? Do you think God cares one way or the other? But He does care about something else. He cares about how we use our free will, the decisions we make moment by moment. That's what builds or destroys character. That's what draws us to Him or away from Him. That's what He cares about. And you better believe that Islam places a tremendous emphasis on that!"

"Thank you."

With two minutes to go, a young man standing in the back was recognized.

"This is for Mrs. Wyatt. Madame, there is never more than one truth. Truth reflects the way things finally are, and that's the *only* way they are. Put all the religions side by side, and only one of them can be right. How can you say God doesn't care what religion you practice? That is saying God doesn't care about the truth. The fact is you have lost your way. You don't even recognize there *is* a truth. I can see what a nice lady you are, but you're leading people to hell. You're not a bad person, you're just confused. May Allah have mercy on you and bring you back to him!"

The young man finished abruptly to much murmuring, and Silas held his breath as he watched Saira mentally gird herself for battle, with only ninety seconds to get the job done. He held Izzy's little hand.

"Sir, please hear me out without interrupting. You have spoken bluntly, and you have given me leave to do the same. You are spouting back what you've been taught since you were a babe. You have not begun to think for yourself. I was once like you. I could even recite by heart much of the Quran. You are correct that truth is one, but it's endlessly complex. As you say, truth reflects the way things are. And, of course, you assume that Islam has it all. That is your mistake. Hindus say that religion is a thousand-faced diamond. You and I see one of the faces, the Christian another, the Hindu another. Study the other religions and climb out of your little box. Then we can talk."

"But you are overlooking the obvious. Why study the other religions when Allah has revealed all the truth we need to know?"

"My young friend, Allah has done no such thing."

"What do you mean? That's blasphemy!"

"Only to Muslims like you. If you had been born to a different religion, as we have seen, it would be a liberating truth."

As the moderator called the meeting to a close, three reporters hurried up to Saira and barraged her with questions. In many communities across America people were asking themselves, "Who is this lady?" while others asked, "Who is this apostate?" Meanwhile Silas, the celebrated syndicated columnist, beamed unobserved off to the side of the room.

From that day on, the Muslim mother of a ten-year-old daughter and one-year-old son embarked on the career she had dreamed of for herself.

# Chapter 18

The new nation of Palestine was born when Israel, under relentless pressure from its allies, handed over control of the West Bank, minus the settlements that it successfully bargained for and was allowed to keep, to the UN. After 130 years of futile bargaining and posturing, the world rested. A week went by without a single terrorist event. But new resentments boiled over when the old Palestinian Authority, led by Hamas, was prevented from relocating from its headquarters in Gaza to the new nation. The Caliphate blamed the prohibition on Israel, when in fact Israel and Palestine were in agreement.

This development gave the American Caliphate a fresh target, and cries rang out that it would "smash every synagogue" and "annihilate every Jew," as one of its leaders in hiding boasted.

Attacks on Brooklyn's Jewish neighborhoods and small businesses occurred almost nightly, and the mayor and governor were at a loss what to do. Finally, they called in the National Guard. In the meantime, New York's Muslim population felt threatened, and many refused to leave their homes. Heartsick, Silas looked on and wondered what he would do if he were the mayor or governor.

One person thought she knew what to do, and that was Professor Layla Haddad of Brooklyn's University of Asmaul Husna. Silas heard about it from one of his Muslim contacts. Supposedly a woman on the faculty was calling for a "counterstrike" whenever a Muslim attacked a Jew. He didn't have the details, but it sounded like the makings of an interesting and possibly helpful column. He texted Layla to see what she might know about it.

"Call me," she replied. "I'm in my office. Or call me at home tonight."

He called her at once. "Layla, it's good to hear from you. How are you?"

"I'm well, Si. And you? And how is Saira? I don't hear from her, but I hear *about* her. She is amazing."

"She certainly is."

"In a way she was my inspiration."

"Oh? How's that?"

"For what my class is doing."

"Are you—and your class—let me guess...the force behind the so-called counterstrike?"

"You guessed right."

"Good for you! What's going on? And is it worth writing about?"

"I *need* you to write about it. I need it to be in the headlines in the *Times*, not just a column on the opinion page. I need the whole world to know."

"My God, tell me more."

"You know that popular kosher restaurant in Borough Park that was bombed two nights ago?"

"Yeah, a horrible tragedy."

"Meet me there tomorrow morning at 8:20. It's on 40th Street, near 12th. I'll be there with my class. Bring a photographer."

A weird scene greeted Silas as he showed up at 8:15 a.m. on a cold, cloudy March day. The blackened, smashed building was cordoned off, and there was Layla and her class of about twenty, mostly women wearing their hijabs, marching outside the tape with their placards held high. "Muslims for Jews," "We condemn the Caliphate," "God loves us all," "Muslims mourn your loss," "The Caliphate are murderers," "Israel is our friend," "Jewish brothers and sisters, forgive us!" and the like drew admiring looks from the mostly Jewish onlookers. Somebody yelled at the marchers for what "you pigs" did, and one old man pulled off one of the marcher's hijabs. But most of the crowd nodded their heads in solidarity.

"This is what we plan on doing," said Layla over a cup of coffee after the "strike" broke up. "These kids are my Senior Seminar class, and we'll go on strike when a Jew is attacked in these neighborhoods."

"Go on strike? Go on strike from what?"

"From the classroom. My class starts at 8:20 a.m. on Monday and Wednesday."

"Got it."

"If you can, Si, paint my little class as a group of heroes. They are standing up to the Caliphate at the risk of their lives. They show the Caliphate that their tactics will lose converts, not gain them. We want to start a movement. We want to be an example to Muslims in other colleges, in other cities. If you make it look heroic enough, young people will flock to it rather than to the Caliphate. Young people are always looking for a cause, and they'll gravitate to the one that asks the most from them. I'm asking my students for their lives. Can you sell this to your boss? Are you excited about it?"

"So you mean to repeat this performance every time there's an attack?"

"That's not possible. There are too many. But once a week is our temporary target. My students understand the risk and they unanimously chose it. And the president of the university fully supports it. He's even thinking about putting the whole university on strike so thousands can march."

"Wow! Please urge him to do that. Can I suggest he do that in my column?"

"Why not?"

"What happens if the Caliphate guns down your students as they march?"

"We've gone over that. At the sound of a shot, we scatter and take cover. But if it's only an egg or a tomato thrown at us, or a hijab pulled off, or a jeer, we try to remember how they've been brainwashed and ignore the insult. But if they really did kill us, I'd organize another class, and that class would march!"

"You can't be serious."

"Do you remember that class on Gandhi back in Chicago? Ever since then I've been convinced nothing good ever happens except on the back of a tragedy. Eventually the murderers can't bear to look at their own crimes. Only then does the world change. Only then will the Caliphate be defeated."

Silas sipped his coffee and looked pensively at the jacketed people passing by outside the window with their frosty breaths. "I don't know," he finally said. "The Caliphate's tactics seem to mummify the souls of their recruits. If you're operating without a conscience, Gandhi just produces fodder for the beasts."

"You can't allow yourself to think that way, Si."

"But you have a child, and you have your students. You have a lot to stay alive for. We both do. So do your students."

She looked out at the same passersby and frowned. "Yes, you have a point. She's something to watch—such a delightful and interesting child. But you're right. For myself death would be easy to accept if it weren't for Safiya. I guess I spoke too...too offhandedly."

Silas wrote the column about Layla's class, and the *Times* lifted it from the opinion page and gave it top billing as "news." Indeed it was news, and even though Layla's university did not go on strike, a few college classes around the country followed the example of her "heroes." Even some Muslim high schools joined in, even one private elementary school in Philadelphia. And the mayhem did seem to quiet for a while—until a device that released poison gas on a flight from LA to DC killed all on board even though the plane was safely guided down by computer to the runway at Dulles. The *New York Daily News* described this latest atrocity as a "flying tomb." The Caliphate openly and immediately took credit for it.

# Chapter 19

For years Saira and Silas talked about writing a book to bring their religions closer together. Both knew that such a project could be dangerous and would have little or no impact on the true believers from either side, but they saw it as a way of bringing moderates closer together. Silas was much less enthusiastic about the book, and he worried that it might compromise his position at the *Times,* but Saira was determined. "Look, Si, somebody needs to do it." They were sitting on the deck in their backyard on a warm autumn evening. "Progress comes when opposite sides work out a compromise, you know that. Christianity and Islam shouldn't be rivals, but each has to give ground. Maybe in three hundred years they'll combine into a single religion."

"That would be nice, but scriptures don't change. The Quran and the Bible will be the same then as now. How can we fix that?"

"Gosh, Mom, you guys are always talking about religion," said Izzy, now fifteen, as she pranced out to the deck from volleyball practice in her black spandex gym suit. "It's simple. Dad has to admit that Jesus was just a man and didn't die on a cross, and you have to admit that we don't have to starve ourselves during Ramadan and pray five times a day and kill people who disagree with us. It's ridiculous."

Silas smiled. "How'd practice go?"

"I got promoted. I grew three inches from last year, no thanks to Mom, and now I'm a hitter. It's fun!"

"Let me put it this way, sweetie. In volleyball some girls are born setters and others are born hitters. It's all in their genes. In religion it's the same. You're born a Christian or a Muslim, depending on your parents. That's the way it is. But that's not the way it has to be. In volleyball you're either tall or short, and you can't change that. But you can change religions, though it's almost never easy. What your Mom and I want to do is make it easier."

"Dad, that's a weird analogy."

"Oh yeah? Can you come up with a better one?"

"Sure. It's like water and ice. They start out different, but they can be melted or frozen into one another. What's so hard about that? And if you don't want to be religious at all, it's like steam. It just blows off."

She looked at her father as if she couldn't imagine how he could be so dumb. Saira suddenly clapped her hands and burst out laughing. And Silas beamed and joined in the mirth with laughter of his own. It pleased him enormously to have such a daughter. And from that day forward he called her, when talking about religion or philosophy, "Miss Analogy."

# Chapter 20

*Cross and Crescent: A Dialog* created the outrage Silas feared. It also brought a fatwa to Saira. She shrugged it off as intimidation. Silas hired a bodyguard anyway and stationed him near the front steps of their home during the short nights of the last week of June 2116. Just in case. There were no incidents, and he released the guard after a week.

Oddly, it was Silas, not Saira, who experienced an attack, but not of a violent kind. He got a call from the Archbishop of New York, Cardinal Steven Nolan. "The Archbishop would be honored to discuss your book with you," said his secretary.

Silas gladly accepted the invitation and immediately went online in search of the proper way of addressing a cardinal. He also ordered a book on the history of the Church since the Third Vatican Council in 2042–43 under Pope Francis II. He had the big picture, but was fuzzy on the details. He wanted to be ready for the cardinal.

What impressed him most was the Church's social agenda. No one was excluded anymore from Holy Communion (the "Blessed Sacrament") because they had been divorced, or were openly gay, or had had an abortion, or practiced birth control, or had married outside the Church, even to a non-Christian. These practices were discouraged, especially abortion, and the Sacrament of Reconciliation strongly recommended. But in the end the Church left these matters up to the individual's conscience after "prayerful consideration." The resolutions on the priesthood he was pretty sure he already knew, but he went over them anyway. The Church continued to recommend a life of celibate service, either male or female, with celibacy a requirement for an archbishop or higher; but married men and women were welcomed to the priesthood. Married homosexuals and transsexuals could become deacons and could perform all priestly functions for a parish under duress or in crisis. And certain Anglicans and Lutherans could become Catholic priests after minimal training.

Then there was Pope Thomas, the first ever by that name. This first U.S. pope, one-quarter Mexican and born and raised in Mobile, Alabama, chose the name Thomas to show his approval of doubt as a necessary rite of passage to a mature Christian faith—this was in the 2070s. This humble man was admired by intellectuals all over the world and won back to Catholicism many who had once judged it hopelessly "medieval." But he was reviled by others, especially conservatives, for almost overseeing "the debacle of the ages," as one of his cardinals called it. The "debacle" was the selling of the Vatican. Thomas was moved to do this for two reasons: the grandeur and opulence of the Vatican never would have met with Jesus's approval, and the Church desperately needed the money to provide a living wage to all the new priests that Vatican III brought with it. The plan failed because the Vatican, including its art treasures, appraised for $266 billion, and the only buyer who could raise even three-quarters of that amount was a consortium of Muslim bankers from fourteen countries. Even then Thomas remained determined. But when it was learned that the great Michelangelo frescoes in the Sistine Chapel would have to be scrubbed out, in keeping with Islam's view of figurative art in sacred space, Thomas gave in. As a result, the Vatican remained in Catholic hands, and most Catholic priests other than pastors and higher-ups worked a side job. Rome's cardinals breathed a collective sigh of relief.

Silas, however, was not content with all this progress, and he was pretty sure his views, which he laid out in his and Saira's book, had come under intense scrutiny from Archbishop Nolan.

Since the meeting was set for Friday afternoon, he was working at the *Times* building. Somehow news of the meeting leaked out, and his writer colleagues razzed him about "going to confession" for his many sins. He was by far the most celebrated of the *Times'* columnists—everybody acknowledged that—but no one would have guessed it by the abuse he sometimes took on Fridays. He was happy to be the butt of a joke and often encouraged it. He had learned how to get along with fellow workers. The NYU experience was behind him.

The cardinal's residence was a two-hundred-year-old neo-Gothic mansion adjoined to St. Patrick's Cathedral. Silas was led into a receiving room with lush scarlet carpeting and priceless antiques and paintings, quite out of keeping with Pope Thomas's bare-bones policies. A large crucifix featuring a white marble Jesus fixed to a jet-black cross seemed out of place. He was told the archbishop would join him as soon as he got off the phone. Fifteen minutes later a portly man wearing the traditional red cassock greeted him with outstretched arms and a hearty hello.

"Your Eminence," said Silas, allowing his hands to be grasped by the bigger man's.

"Forgive me for making you wait, but I was on the phone with the Pope."

"Oh! Well, I hope—"

"Just kidding. It was just my dear old mother, and she was convinced it was my birthday. Actually it's *her* birthday! Anyway, I've asked you here to talk about your book. Here, take a seat."

They sat facing each other in chairs with scarlet cushioning to match the carpets.

"I understand you're a Catholic. May I call you Silas?"

"Please do."

"I was happy to see you on the St. Patrick's register. Do you live near here?"

"No, I live in North Bronx, but my work at the *Times* is close by."

"Do you attend Mass here?"

"Actually, almost never, but I often sit in the Cathedral to pray—in my own peculiar way. I love to sit quietly in the Lady

Chapel, out of the way of all the tourists."

"Yes, a wonderful place to adore the Blessed Sacrament."

"Yes, it is, though that's not quite what I do."

"I gathered that from your book," said the cardinal with a wily grin.

"The monstrance is a wonderful focal point for concentrated prayer, but I turn inward to find God. Not that I have a very definite idea of who or what God is. But at my soul's center is a tiny chip of divinity, so to speak. Sinking down into those quiet depths is what I mean by prayer."

"You speak like a mystic."

"I'm no mystic. It's quite beyond me, barring a miracle."

"Well, I'm not either." The cardinal laughed in a good-natured way. "Though, like you, I work at it. But don't you see? That's where the Church can be of such help. The Church gives us a God we can talk to, a God for the masses, and plenty of saints and angels to help along the way. And the Blessed Mother, who carries our prayers to her Son, the God-man Jesus. In your book I missed this."

"Yes, I'm afraid you did. Though I like the way you put it just now."

"Silas, I understand the reason you wrote your book. It's to show where Islam went wrong and—"

"I would put that differently, Your Eminence. My wife—"

"Please, dispense with the formality. You influence the world as much as I anyway. Call me Steve. Let's be friends. Equal to equal."

"Thank you...Steve. But my influence surely falls vastly short of yours. My wife and I, I was saying, wrote the book to bring the two religions closer together. And remember—she's a Muslim. Really, I'm under no illusion of ever bringing Islam under the sway of our faith. All I want to do is show where they're similar and where they...and where they, I'll speak bluntly, where they're wrong and can give ground, and where *we're* wrong and should give ground."

"Yes, I picked up on that, and that's what I especially want to talk to you about. I think you give way too much ground to the Muslim on the question of Christ's divinity. Do you really think that's negotiable?"

"I hope it is. Because there's nothing so offensive to the Muslim as—they'd put it this way—as setting up a 'partner to God.' And Jesus is that partner. To them this is a damnable sin. It's the main reason they feel they've got to defeat us—not work alongside us as a kindred religion—but defeat us. If we'd give up that claim, half the battle would be won. World peace might be just around the corner."

"I hear you well, Silas, but giving up Jesus's divinity would lead to denying the Trinity. We would all be Arians!"

Silas wriggled in his chair. He sensed the impasse, beyond which there was no going. He wilted in his chair and said meekly, "Your Eminence, I see your love of the Church and all the faithful. I share this with you. I never intended my book to be read by devout Catholics happy with what they have. I intended it for thoughtful Christians who were willing to think outside the box for the good of the world."

"And you made it clear you can't accept the Nicene Creed," the archbishop continued. "Jesus as both fully God and fully man, the virgin birth, the Resurrection, Christ's atonement for our sins, Mary as the Mother of God, most of our Creed. I found myself wondering, frankly, how you could consider yourself a Christian."

"It's true I'm not a Christian in the sense you mean. But if you use Jesus's own words, then I'd like to think I qualify. He told us the most important thing was to follow the two Great Commandments: to love God with all our strength and our neighbor as ourselves. And he told us how to do this in his great Sermon on the Mount: feed the hungry, clothe the naked, forgive our enemies, turn the other cheek, all that wonderful stuff. There's nothing like it in all the world's scriptures. I'm not a creedal Christian. I'm a Great Commandments Christian. And I think that's the best way to be a Christian."

"A 'Great Commandments Christian.' A nice phrase. A catchy phrase. In your own way you're a man of God, I grant that. But you're not a Christian by traditional standards, Silas, and it troubles me to see you being taken as one. You're ignoring the entire history of what came *after* Christ."

"Intentionally. Yes, I am."

"You seem to be trying to reform the religion, but you're an outsider. Reform must come from inside. From within the club, so to speak. Otherwise you'd be crashing the party."

Silas watched as a cat he hadn't noticed sauntered up to him from somewhere. "Hello, kitty," he said. Then looking back up at the cardinal, he said. "Was Martin Luther King an insider, a member of the club? As I see it, it's the outsider that brings reform. And I wouldn't mind being that outsider, along with my wife. It's true: we are reformers. We are trying to reform our religions. She lays out the steps she thinks Islam has to take, and I lay them out for the Christian. If only the world would listen."

"Ah, my friend, the world will not listen, unless you go and get yourself killed. Then it might. Just a little."

They talked on, discovered much they agreed on, but never came to an agreement on the crucial question of Christ's nature. They enjoyed each other's company, and it pained each of them to part with hearts entwined but intellects so far apart.

# Chapter 21

Rumors of sex slavery surfaced in New Medina, the posh new city built by Muslims for Muslims in Florida's panhandle. Three teenage girls came forth to tell a story of kidnapping and repeated rape by their "owners." Trafficking in sex wasn't exactly hot news in a world saturated with it, but when U.S. Muslims were caught practicing it, and claimed they were "drawing closer to God" by the act, Saira took note.

"There it is again!" she practically shouted at Silas as they watched the evening news. "I've spoken out against it so many times, yet they don't seem to hear. They quote the Quran completely out of context. What can I do?"

"Count your successes. These guys will be tried and convicted."

"Sure, and then serve a short sentence because they claim they were practicing their religion, and everybody is so freaked out about Islamophobia they go soft. These monsters ought to have the tips of their fingers cut off!"

"Saira, where did you get that?"

"It's in the Quran. It's a punishment reserved for nonbelievers. Okay, maybe just the tip of every *other* finger."

"But they *are* believers," he said, looking slightly amused by her outburst.

Suddenly she became reflective. "Seriously, Si, I've got to do something about this. Something I've never done before."

She wanted to see for herself what it involved. And there was no better theater for it than the Sudan. Silas adamantly opposed the plan and would have gone with her if it weren't for the children. "You might end up a victim yourself!" he said.

"I owe it to my followers, even to the country. I've got to describe the horror in full detail. I need to get close to it, personally close."

"But others have already done that, many times."

"No. They've only interviewed the victims, not the perpetrators, the organizers. I have to see it for myself. And that's not possible here."

She promised to give him a detailed description on her cell phone. "I'll tell them I'm recruiting for the Caliphate in America and want to see firsthand what sells. They'll believe me." They both set up phony accounts with pseudonyms to protect themselves. He promised not to text back. She bought a "wipe-out app" that deleted her texts with no record of their ever being sent as soon as they were read or viewed. "Make sure you forward them to your personal account before they disappear so we don't lose them," she added.

Sudanese men from the north had been capturing or paying others to capture women from South Sudan since the two countries split over a hundred years ago. The Quran forbade Muslim males from enslaving Muslims, but Christians and animists, according to the Caliphate, were fair game if it became clear they were enemies of Islam. Slavery had been outlawed throughout Africa since the late twentieth century, but the practice continued anyway, and with impunity in Sudan.

"Arrived in Khartoum. Sudan Airways not bad. Food good." This was her first text.

Next day: "Taking plane to Kadugli, near border with South Sudan. Strange smells. Arid landscape turning green as we fly south. I'm wearing a *tob*, a long piece of cloth wrapped around my body, covers me down to my ankles. Beautiful designs and colors. Shorts and blouse underneath. Head tie, African style, no hijab, on head."

Later: "Arrived in Kadugli, green and lovely after rainy season. All-Muslim city of 140,000. No church anywhere. Contacted imam at main mosque. He was suspicious. Sympathized with the Caliphate. Scary guy."

Next day just before going to bed: "Hotel has air-conditioning but at quite a price. Found local Caliphate headquarters. Told a subaltern I was a recruiter from USA. Missing you."

Early next morning: "They call sex slaves concubines. All very respectable. Common practice among Arab elites. Hypocrites! Meeting in an hour. Love you."

Saira finished breakfast and walked for twenty minutes over to Headquarters, not knowing what to expect. She was pleased to see that "the Chief," as he was called, was waiting for her, not a flunky. Kamal el-Hashem looked to be a man of about sixty in good health, with a neatly trimmed beard and bald head. He was an Arab. His spacious office showed signs of sophisticated taste, with a few antiques mounted on stands and a beautifully carved coffee table off to the side of the room with two brocade arm chairs keeping it company. The man himself sat behind a large mahogany desk with an immaculate glass top. Behind him hung the Sudanese flag, with its green triangle, the traditional color of Islam, sharing space with a tricolor of red, white, and black. On the wall to his right hung two woolen tapestries that brightened the room with displays of intertwined ivy and flowers. On the other side a map of the two Sudans, north and south, showing their major towns and cities, hung by a cord. Next to it, handsomely framed, hung a map of the Sudan before it was divided a century earlier. Saira noticed this oddity right away when she was ushered in and wondered what it meant. The Chief did not rise to meet her or offer his hand.

After a rather curt greeting, el-Hashem got down to business. His English was passable. "I hear you come here to study our customs. You are American and want to see how we recruit. You ask about sex. From a woman this seems very strange. Do you know the meaning of my name, el-Hashem? The Crusher."

"Sir, the Sudanese are noted all across the world for their concubinage. You have perfected the art. Concubines attract recruits. I want to see how this works."

"You honor us, but do you want to see men in—the act?" His eyebrows shot upward when he said, "the act."

She was embarrassed and wondered if the question was designed to intimidate her. "Of course not, sir! I am a writer and a speaker, and my words must be vivid. I like to speak of things I have seen, but *not that!*"

"Before we go further, I must ask you to recite the first six verses of the Quran."

At this demand Saira sensed real danger for the first time since she entered the country, but the words came easily to her.

"And now—remove your *tob.*"

"What? Sir, I am a Muslim!"

"Madame, you are a Muslim unlike any I know. You have clothing under, yes?"

Saira was aghast and stared back at him, not knowing what to do.

"Madame, I must 'take precautions,' as they say."

Saira unwound the *tob* and stood in front of el-Hashem in a sleeveless blouse, wet with sweat around the bust, and shorts that ended just above the knees.

"I see you have a cell phone," he said. He must have noticed the lump it made in the side pocket of her shorts. She almost panicked. That last message to Si, what was it? Then she remembered: "They call sex slaves concubines. All very respectable. Common practice among Arab elites. Hypocrites!"

"I need to see your cell phone."

As she fidgeted with the phone getting it out of her pocket, two thoughts knifed through her mind: *Should I excuse myself and make a quick exit, or should I hand it over?* She calculated the time back home: 9:00 a.m. in Sudan translated to—to what? A quick tally came to 5:00 p.m. Would Si have read the message between 4:00 and 5:00 p.m.?

She calculated the odds and handed the phone over to the Chief, and as he played with it, she remembered how Si warned her she might herself become a victim. One hour. *One hour to eternity* ran through her mind. If he hadn't read it, if he'd been napping or turned his phone off, the message was still waiting for him—and waiting for Chief Kamal el-Hashem, "the Crusher."

"There is nothing here," he said.

She gulped and said, "No, sir, I carry it only for an emergency."

"You do not use it like everybody else?"

"For security reasons, no, I don't. Not while I travel. Not while I travel for the Caliphate. The UN has its headquarters here, right? One must take precautions, as you say."

"Not even your husband?"

"Not even for him."

Puzzled, he studied her, then said, "How can I be of help?"

He had fallen for her ruse. Calming herself, she said, "I would like to talk to the recruits, then to the concubines. Can you arrange this?"

He shuffled in his chair and frowned. "On Friday afternoon, after prayers, we expose criminals. Beheadings, hangings, crucifixions, stonings, amputations, lashing, all on display. This week we have a case of rape. A man's sister was raped. The perpetrator will watch his own sister, a virgin, raped by one of our top recruits. We will force him to watch. You may interview the recruit when he is finished. He is South African, and black."

"His own virgin sister? Isn't that harsh?"

"It is harsh. And that is why there are so few rapes in the Sudan. It deters."

"But that's not quite the same as what I was hoping to see."

"You are correct, but it is close. Many concubines come from the Christian south. They are dark-skinned, black. They are not only infidels, but inferior infidels. We capture them, sell them to the highest bidder, and use the money to feed the hungry and take care of widows. Best of all, most of them convert to Islam.

Everybody wins. So it is better than what you will see. But it is the same."

With well-disguised revulsion, Saira said, "Yes, I see what you mean. Excellent. Excellent! Can I meet with some of these lucky concubines from the south?"

El-Hashem considered. "You can, but they do not understand English."

"Can you find a translator?"

The Chief stared at the map of the undivided Sudan and tapped a pen against his glass-topped desk. "I have a better idea," he finally said. "I will call you at the hotel."

That afternoon to pass the time Saira hiked out into the countryside. Livestock grazed in lush unfenced fields. At one point she found a tree to relieve herself behind. As she squatted, there was a frightening hiss. A snake was no more than a foot from her bare bottom. Inch by inch she rotated her hip away from the snake without rising, then slowly rose. It was the second time in a day she had dodged death.

The Chief kept his word and had, not just one, but three recruits waiting for her in an annex to a training camp at the city's edge. Along with the South African were a Canadian and a Brit, both of mixed race. The South African's name was Matthew. He came from a family devoid of any religion.

Each identified himself by name and age. The oldest was twenty-one. Saira explained what she wanted from them, and they looked embarrassed, even disbelieving. "Speak openly," she said. "I'm forty-five years old, married, and have two children." Then she lied, "Both boys, one nineteen, the other seventeen. I want them to be willing to die for the Caliphate, just as I am — and you are. But they are reluctant. What drew you to join? Was the promise of sexual partners a big draw? I understand two of you have been matched, and that you, Matthew, were honored with a special prize yesterday. Please tell me: has sex been all you expected?"

Each of them looked at the others. Finally the Canadian, Fiza, the oldest, spoke up. "This is not something we talk about with a woman."

"Do not think of me as a woman!" Saira flashed back. "Think of me as a representative of the American wing of the Caliphate. I *order* you to speak up, and speak truthfully. No one in Kadugli will hear what you say. Trust me as you would your own mother."

Fiza looked to the left at his suddenly chastened colleagues, then began: "Sex is forbidden until marriage in the Muslim culture I grew up in. Guys are wanting it, but they are scared. But the Caliphate says it's good and that Allah approves of it. So they gave us—we call them slaves. And that's what they are. Black Christians from the south. Yeah, it's good. I enjoy it. But I expected something better. And my slave hates me. I can tell. So it's not so good."

Saira waited a moment, then asked Selim, the Brit, if he had anything to say. She could see the muscles above his cheeks pulsing. He looked as if he were about to explode. Finally he spit out, "My fucking slave is pregnant! So I can't have sex for six more months. It's forbidden. So I'm stuck with this stinking whore who has my child. They forced me to marry her. No, it's not what I imagined, not at all!"

Again Saira waited. She was shocked by Selim's honesty. She wondered what he would have said if he hadn't felt observed, policed. She wondered if he would have dared to speak so freely if she had been a man. Perhaps her motherly promise had broken through his pretenses, and he had risked his life. One more to go: would it too be a confession? "What about you, Matthew?"

The young man shook his head rapidly, almost frantically, as if he wanted to shake the memory of what he'd done out of existence. Then he spoke in a voice that shook with emotion. "Oh my God. That poor girl. I hated what I did. I prayed to Allah to bless what I was about to do, then I prayed to Allah to forgive me for what I did. She was only thirteen, and she was dry as a bone. She screamed and screamed. She said it hurt and begged me to stop. But I just dug into her. Oh my God, it was horrible! And she was white. That made it all the worse for her. That's why they chose me, not because I was their star recruit. But the Boss said it was good for her to suffer. It was Allah's will."

A silence followed, a silence of remorse and shame, and Saira let the silence swallow them up. Then she asked, "Matthew, are you saying the sex incentive is phony? That it's bad bait?"

"Please, Ma'am, don't tell anyone what I said. They'll kill me."

"I have already told you your secrets will die with me. You are safe. But I have to know. Was it mainly the promise of sex that brought you here? Or was it something else? Selim, what do you say to that?"

"It was a lot of things, but sex was cool, definitely cool."

"Was it cool for you too, Fiza?"

Fiza struggled to say what he felt. Then, "Tell your kids to stay away from all this shit. I miss home. I never thought I'd say that."

Saira felt moved to tears for Fiza. She wanted to gather him up in a mother's hug. But she kept a straight face and let it appear she was disappointed.

She left them with a final promise not to reveal anything they had said.

Eleanor Siddig was waiting for Saira at one of the city's neighborhood mosques. Both women wore the traditional tob and head tie. Most striking about Eleanor was her blonde hair and blue eyes. She might have been a Swede if Saira hadn't known better. They met in a plain, undecorated side room on plastic chairs around a cheap round table.

Saira knew nothing about Eleanor except that she was the second wife of a wealthy cattle rancher and leather maker. Saira didn't introduce herself as a recruiter for the Caliphate, and she had no hint as to Eleanor's politics. To all appearances, two women from different worlds were meeting as strangers just to get acquainted.

As women do, and generally do with so much more grace than men, boundaries were erased almost on sight. Eleanor was thrilled to find a woman who spoke English, and Saira, with her usual curiosity piqued, wondered why the Chief chose this woman for her to meet. "How did you happen to end up in Kadugli, of all places?" she began. "And do I detect a faint Irish accent?"

That was all it took, and Eleanor's eyes glowed with the prospect of telling her story. "My father and mother were missionaries from County Waterford. They came to South Sudan not to convert but to serve. One day, when I was seventeen, I was upset because my mom wouldn't let me wear her dress on a date with a Christian boy. I walked alone on the main road out toward the fields and was so angry that I told God to let me get kidnapped to punish my mother. And that's exactly what happened. I was taken with other slaves to Kadugli in the back of a truck. The man whose name I bear, Mr. Siddig, bought me at auction. I was just a concubine, a slave, but he liked me so much he eventually took me as his second wife. I have had three children by him. I'm twenty-four. How about you?"

"Me? I'm an American woman, a Muslim, with two children of my own. And a Christian husband. But please, tell me a little more. Have you ever seen your parents since this happened? Do they know where you are?"

"No, how could they?"

"That's terrible. How have you dealt with this?"

"At first, like any other slave, I wept constantly. I hated everything about the man who bought me and raped me, almost every night. But after I became pregnant, he left me alone. But I was bored out of my mind, and then he brought me books in English.

Many books, but censured. And he tutored me in the Quran, its teachings. And he forced me to convert. And I did, but not in my heart. And I had more children."

"Do you love this man?"

She looked around the room, as if suspecting a spy. "Can I speak frankly? Do you promise not to tell?" she whispered.

"By God's holy name, I promise. You are absolutely safe with me."

"I hate the man, but love the children he has given me. But he does not know I hate him. Nobody does, except you. Oh, it is good to get this out! Everybody thinks I'm a happy Muslim housewife. Oh, if only they knew! But they must never know."

"Eleanor, this is appalling, appalling, and I weep for you in my heart." Saira held out her hands, and Eleanor took them with tears beginning to flow. Moved to her depths, Saira could not resist the urge to confess her own deceit to this young Christian mother. She knew she was risking her life, but she felt safe anyway. Still holding her hands, she said, "Eleanor, can I now speak frankly? Do you promise, solemnly promise, not to tell anyone what I tell you now?"

Surprised, Eleanor said, "I do promise."

"Like you, I'm not what I seem. I'm not in sympathy with the kind of Islam that has done this to you. I'm a devout Muslim, but I'm committed to destroying the Caliphate and all it represents. I've come here to see what it does to its victims, both slaves like you and the young men they recruit. I'm here to expose it, not promote it. I'm a spy, a spy for true Islam. Eleanor, tell me where you were kidnapped. What's the name of the town? What are your parents' names? I'll do everything I can to get you reunited with your people."

Eleanor broke into violent sobbing, then controlled herself and said, still holding Saira's hands, "No, you must not! They'll kill my children before giving them up to be raised as Christians. I must be content. Someday I'll be reunited with my people—in heaven."

"Are you sure? But you'll have to watch your children brought up in a religion not your own. How can you bear that?"

"Our God is the same. I'll teach them to love this God and love their enemies, as Christ taught us. With that I must be content. And I am."

By now Saira was fighting back tears of her own. She let loose Eleanor's hands so she could embrace her. She held her for a long time, then released her and said, "Eleanor, let's never forget this moment. I love you as my own daughter. I'll be waiting for you in heaven along with your parents, when you come over, and my heart will be bursting with joy!"

That evening the Chief called her at her hotel and congratulated her on seeing the wonderful impact that "concubinage at its best" can have. Saira thanked him and said she had achieved, with his "immense help," new insights into its virtues. That night she dared to text Silas one more time before slipping away from Kadugli without fanfare the next morning. She typed, "Amazing contacts. Great story for your next column. Am considering an acting career! (Not really.) Your loving Saira."

# Chapter 22

Within a few days of Saira's fifty-first birthday, the British Parliament proposed a law prohibiting the five daily calls to prayer, or *salat*. British non-Muslims outnumbered Muslims 60 percent to 40 percent. The majority argued that the first call to prayer, at dawn, interfered with sleep, especially among the elderly. Others claimed that the "eerie" sounds of the prayer, called out from amplifiers all over the country, were alien or even offensive to the British ear. Others pointed out the obvious: a free app announcing the times of the prayer could be installed on anyone's smartphone, and the only reason Muhammad instituted the call to prayer was that he didn't have a phone. Taking it one step further, the critics argued that the blaring sounds of the muezzin's voice were nothing more than a tactic used by the Caliphate for cramming Islam down the throats, or rather into the ears, of nonbelievers. Fighting back, Muslims reminded Christians that the bells in some of their churches rang out every quarter hour—at which point, in the endless debate, Christians reminded Muslims that the bells did not announce any doctrine like the salat's "I testify that there is no God but Allah," and that furthermore the bells were musical, not religious. Ultimately the argument that convinced Parliament, which had disestablished Anglicanism as the state religion in 2067 and in other ways adopted the U.S. model, was that the *salat* violated the separation of church and state.

The Caliphate responded immediately with a widespread bombing campaign, especially aimed at members of Parliament and their families. To help quell the violence, Parliament adopted the conciliatory plan of inviting leading Muslims from around the world to a "peace conference" in London. Saira had gained worldwide celebrity status when word leaked out what she had done in the Sudan; thus, she was one of those invited—

one of eight altogether, half of them thought to be conservative, half progressive.

Silas made plans for his recently widowed mother to stay in their home with Izzy and Eliot, now sixteen and seven, and flew over to support his wife and, as he frankly admitted to his boss at the *Times*, take a little vacation. He and Saira planned a self-guided, week-long, ninety-seven-mile walking tour of the beautiful Lake Country to the north after her speech.

The speeches were staged in ancient, hundred-year-old London Stadium, which had just undergone renovation in time for a week-long World Peace Concert. Saira's speech laid out her plan for compromise, a plan that she and Silas had been talking over for weeks. Sitting unrecognized and well outside the VIP gallery near the speaker's platform in the immense oval stadium, he marveled at what Saira had become. How had she done it? By taking risks and never resting until she had achieved her goal, that was how. Every morning she got up before the kids; she stepped into the garden, picked a flower (if available), and placed it in a small bowl of water on a makeshift stand in the computer room. Then she said her prayers and vowed that she would be "the best version of herself" that she could be for that day. And for her that meant never stopping until she had accomplished the day's task. Procrastination was anathema to her. When she failed at her task, as rarely happened, she could be hard to live with. She was a FORCE, charming and more beautiful than ever. She painted her fingernails and had her hair washed, blown out, colored, and styled. She knew how to look good and thought it important to look good in order to accomplish her mission. He sometimes teased her about her "vanity" but did nothing to discourage it—he liked the finished product too much. And now there she was on one of the world's biggest stages, speaking from behind a bulletproof plastic shield, with the King of England in attendance. Amazing! It humbled him to think she might be leaving a bigger imprint on the world than he.

They traveled light. Contours, the company that delivered their luggage from one inn to the next while they hiked with a light pack, supplied them with maps and directions. They walked from village to village, climbing fences and crossing fields, keeping company with sheep and cattle, admiring the immaculately kept gardens that fronted many of the homes, stopping to read inscriptions on unvisited tombs surrounding the little churches. On one occasion they looked inside a tiny church from which a sound came—a charming mini-Gothic structure with Mass going on. Three ancient women, too crippled to kneel, and a white-whiskered priest intoned their prayers to a God who listened to an ever-dwindling number of British Christian petitions.

The scene touched them both as they thought ahead to their own fates, now nearer to them than their births. They walked on and up, paused to eat their bagged lunches, and walked up some more. At the crest of a wind-scoured mountain they came across a marker embedded on a rock which told of a place where William Wordsworth and his brother John had hiked to. The poet immortalized that lonely, chilly, treeless place with its tiny purple flowers because it was where he last saw his brother alive; they had departed, Wordsworth for his home in Grasmere, his brother for heaven, so the plaque said. "That'll be our fate too," said Saira. "Look," she added, "the same tiny purple flowers growing out of the moss. Those flowers, so like us, tiny, insignificant."

Silas, shivering in his thin jacket, stared down at his phone and dropped down on the lee side of the rock. "Over here," he called out. "Gosh it's cold!" It was beginning to mist, and Saira snuggled up against him while rubbing her hands. "Look," he said. "You get special mention in the *London Times*. This guy really liked your proposal. I might be insignificant, but *you're* not."

"How about that? Hmm…he even got it right."

"He did. But the polls, on both sides, are less enthusiastic. Look at this."

She read the article and said, "Aha, but they're not throwing bricks either!"

They knew that Muslims would hate having the *salat* limited to a single call at noon Friday, but her proposal to lift all restrictions at the beginning and end of the holy month of Ramadan mollified them. Her advice to Christians, since she was an outsider, was more problematic, and she and Silas had batted the proposal around over many a cup of coffee. They both knew that Christians would hate not hearing the great bells of St. Paul's and many other churches throughout the country ring in the quarter hour, but Muslims resented the practice—and not just the Caliphate. In her speech she called for "special, even heroic, understanding. For any compromise to work, all must suffer," she told the crowd of 80,000. She called for the practice of quarter-hour ringing to end but, to the relief of many, endorsed the ringing of bells to announce the beginning of a service, including the greatly loved "change ringing." But what won over her Christian audience was two concessions: Big Ben atop Westminster Palace should continue to ring in the hour since it was more a symbol of freedom than of religion, and, as she put it, "on Christmas and Easter, let your bells ring out all day long over the land!" Many Christians learned to trust her as a result.

As they walked down the other side of the mountain toward Grasmere on a stony path weaving through heather, they hardly noticed the landscape. Saira couldn't let die Si's claim that he was less significant than she. "That's simply not true. You think this because you've been doing the same thing too long. You told me last year a million readers had commented on your columns. That's insignificant? Si, you've got the itch for politics. I don't think it's a smart itch, but you've got it. And I think you ought to follow through with it."

"It's too late, love. I'm fifty-six. And it takes money to win an election, gobs of it. Besides, what's out there for me to win? One of fifty-one seats on the City Council? The representative from Spuyten Duyvil? I'm sorry, but I'm just a big picture kind of guy."

"I know you are. And your writing proves it week by week. There's hardly a country in the world you're not familiar with. I bet you won all those geography quizzes in the fifth grade—you know, the ones where you had to name the capitals in South America. What's the capital of Paraguay?"

Silas chuckled and said, "Asunción."

"See? You're a big picture kind of guy, Si, and you'd make a great—what? A great president, but..." and her voice drifted off as the wind whipped the heather close around them.

"Look," she continued, "let's have Ethan over before he dies and pick his brain. He believes in you."

"He's not dying."

"But you are—inside—and it hurts me to watch it."

They arrived in Grasmere, got reunited with their luggage at their inn, and did a little research on Wordsworth before visiting the home where he and his sister, Dorothy, lived. Silas was struck by how vital to Wordsworth's success his sister was—right down to some of the great nature scenes he described. It occurred to him that Saira was to him what Dorothy was to her brother.

"You're the greatest, sweetheart," he told her as they got ready for bed that night.

"I am? I like that word *sweetheart*," she said, flashing a beckoning smile at him. For all the beauty of devoted sibling love, that night, in a small room with a low ceiling in the middle of England's storied Lake Country, Saira and Silas celebrated a different kind of love, though which one is ultimately superior has been debated by philosophers.

# Chapter 23

A little over a month later, in early June, a number of events converged that would change Silas's life forever. First, Parliament sided with Saira's proposal, and the call to prayer was restricted to noon daily, with no sermon added on, as was the custom in some of Britain's more Muslim neighborhoods in the larger cities; the proposal to allow five calls at the beginning and end of Ramadan was endorsed. Second, the new restrictions, to the surprise of almost everyone, produced a period of calm, and Brits rejoiced. But on June 4 a computer attack crippled the guidance systems of London's ambulance corps. Normally an ambulance would magnetically clear away traffic in its way, or if this was impossible, rise over the congestion and reach its destination airborne. Following the attack, ambulances behaved like any other pod stuck in traffic. It took engineers four days to disable the virus, and by that time 630 residents, according to the most reliable estimate, died waiting for help. The Caliphate took credit and warned that New York, which was considering similar restrictions on the call, would be next. Third, the leading Independent candidate for Mayor of New York City dropped out with only five months before the election, and left only a Democrat and a Republican with any chance of winning. Finally, "Uncle E," as Izzy and Eliot called Ethan, was coming to dinner, and Saira had secretly prepped Ethan on Silas's state of mind. "Si's got the best job in the world, but he's burnt out."

At eighty-one Uncle E had been adopted as the family patriarch, and Eliot especially looked forward to his visits. "Can you take us around the block in your flyaway, Uncle E? Jimmy wants to see what it's like." Jimmy was, according to most psychologists, an "imaginary friend," though Silas, and of course Eliot himself, had other ideas.

Ethan was well acquainted with Jimmy, so he played along.

"Sure, but I thought spirits could fly by themselves."

"No, all they can do is fly home to heaven. We just want to go around the block before it gets dark."

"Oh, I see. Well, you tell Jimmy I'll give him a rain check."

"What's a rain check?"

"Check with Jimmy. See if he knows."

Eliot turned aside and asked Jimmy in an ordinary voice if he knew. Then he turned back and said, "He says it means next time."

"What a clever friend you have!" said Uncle E. "I'll bring him into the firm when he grows up."

"Oh no, Uncle E, he's a spirit. And he'll have to grow up over there." Eliot spoke these words with such seriousness that all the adults could do was smile and quietly marvel.

The whole family had worked together on the meal. Silas brewed up one of his famous chicken dishes, this time an exotic, out-of-season dish called Chicken and Peaches Orientale. Saira's specialty was pilafs, and she could make them in her sleep. Izzy meantime was the baker, and for her all-American taste buds there was nothing like a cherry pie topped with vanilla ice cream. As for Eliot and Uncle E, they crumpled lettuce into a big bowl and added tomatoes and avocado. Somewhere in the middle of all this commotion, Jimmy, according to Eliot, retired to heaven.

The meal was served on an oval table covered with antique lace. Saira hadn't forgotten to light candles, and Silas said a blessing and toasted Ethan for "not retiring." Halfway through the meal, Ethan asked Silas if he still had political ambitions.

"Political ambitions? When did I ever have political ambitions? I'm a realist. I just had political *dreams*," said Silas. "But for quite a while, as you know, I've wondered if I missed my true calling. Anyway, I'm not a lawyer, and I'm just too old to start a new career."

"Like hell you are! Remember Ronald Reagan? He was an actor with no political experience when he was elected president.

He was almost seventy."

"Seriously, Ethan, what makes you think I'd make a half-decent politician?"

"You don't have to be. In fact, it'd be better if you weren't. Let me lay it out for you, my boy. Listen very carefully. I'm talking about the mayor's race. Yes, the mayor's race. I assume you'll agree with me Perez has a lock on the Republican nomination, and he's so thick with his fellow Christians that no Muslim will vote for him. And Ahmadi is probably going to win the Democratic nomination in a runoff, and no Christian will vote for him. But then there are all the seculars and religious minorities, and Jasmine Gupta was looking like their girl as an Independent until she dropped out last week. Christ, Si, there's this huge hole—don't you see? You'd pick up all the seculars and maybe a pretty good chunk of the religious because you'd come across as a moderate. And with Saira's recent fame, and her getting out and campaigning for you as Islam's true friend—which you are—I can see a lot of Ahmadi's base turning on him and voting for you. Don't underestimate the glamor factor."

"Glamor factor?" said Saira. "I'll have to remember that one."

"So you're saying I should run as an Independent," said Si. "Isn't this getting a little ridiculous?"

"Not at all. Jasmine dropping out was totally unexpected, and for you it's a bonanza. If you played your cards right, you'd unseat Perez and Ahmadi and be in Gracie Mansion with your family next January."

"That'd be fun, Dad," grinned Izzy as she lapped up the wad of ice cream on her cherry pie.

All eyes were on Silas as silence settled over him. He wore a bemused half smile. He shrugged his shoulders and said, looking at Saira, "What do you think? Isn't one celebrity per family enough?"

"I'd be happy to campaign for you." She reached out and took his hand, which was holding a dessert fork.

"I would too," said Izzy.

"I would too," chimed in Eliot.

"Hey, this has been fun," Silas conceded, "but it takes a political machine and tens of millions of dollars to win an election of this magnitude. Would you pass me the ice cream, Izzy?"

It was at this moment that Ethan fixed that mesmerizing stare of his on Silas and let him know he wasn't kidding. "Silas, there is a $28,500 cap on donations. That's pretty generous. You've got five months until the election. There's enough time if you get busy right away. You should begin by declaring your candidacy in your next column with all the reasons given. You need to select your campaign manager right away, and I'd suggest Jasmine's. He could use a new job. And I'll find a way to cover the expenses that contributions don't."

"Legally?"

"Trust me. I'll find a way. And it would give me something worthwhile to do with my life besides making money."

It was as much Silas's love for his dear old friend that persuaded him to go along with a plan that he thought bordered on madness. So it was settled. Silas wrote his column, filed for candidacy as an Independent, and took a leave of absence from his job at the *Times*. "I'll be back in a couple of months," he told his boss, "so don't clear out my desk."

In spite of his estimate of his chances of winning, Silas threw himself into the fracas with the zeal of a missionary fresh out of seminary. Wagner, his campaign manager, made the adjustment from one candidate to another in less than a week. And Ethan brazenly put in calls to his friends all over the globe. The money started to pour in, and Silas suddenly found himself believing in his chances, and what had been a dream was mutating into an ambition. Over the years he had written countless articles about all the ways the country, and more especially New York City, could change the world for the better, and always his idealism fell on deaf political ears. Now he was in a position to—just maybe—make those changes himself. It was a thrilling prospect. And Saira was as thrilled as Silas. He began to think that, with her help, he could prevail.

# Chapter 24

As the candidates debated what to do about the call to prayer in their city, the Caliphate stepped up its harassment. Justin Perez's home on Staten Island was firebombed in spite of being under heavy guard, and several death threats reached Suleiman Ahmadi's campaign headquarters from Christians aligned with Perez. Both men won their party's nomination and avoided a primary runoff. Now in mid-September, the ballots were set. Perez was the Christian candidate, Ahmadi the Muslim, and Silas non-aligned. In addition, there were a few minor candidates with no chance of winning. One of the questions the pundits debated among themselves was whether Silas's non-aligned posture would help or hurt him at the polls. A writer at the *Post* compared him to a chameleon. Another at the *Daily News* compared him to the crow's eye, which, according to a legend coming out of ancient India, rolled back and forth from the left socket to the right, depending on the need. On the other side, his defenders described him as balanced, the "voice of compromise," even "the city's, and indeed the nation's, only hope." The *Times* stood solidly behind him. And so, surprisingly, did his old friend Cardinal Stephen Nolan.

On September 17 the weekly Quinnipiac poll showed Ahmadi at 36 percent, Perez at 33 percent, Silas at 22 percent, and the remainder either undecided or voting for one of the minor candidates. Silas's backers were sobered but not discouraged, at least not openly. Silas himself asked his God for peace of mind regardless of the outcome. He reminded himself that in the very long run it was the idea that determined the deed, and that writers like him might after all make a difference. Whenever he tended to forget this lesson from history, Saira reminded him of it. It gave him solace and helped him stay sane as the final weeks wound down.

WCBS-TV lined up a two-hour debate on October 1 in prime time featuring the three leading candidates. The most recent Marist Poll, to no one's surprise, showed that the number-one concern of New Yorkers—the figure stood at 94 percent among respondents who described themselves as anti-Caliphate—was their personal safety. So the primary focus of the debate was Islam. The economy, health, tax reform, affordable housing, food and water supplies, parks and recreation, trash collection, the decaying infrastructure, public transportation, stronger dikes to keep out the rising sea, immigration, the prison system, and a few other concerns briefly surfaced. Schools might also have been hastily passed over until Silas spoke up. For him public school policy was a fundamental part of the solution to the Caliphate problem.

Neither Ahmadi nor Perez took Silas seriously—he was too far behind. They went after each other, each attacking the other's morality. Perez described Ahmadi as "too cozy with the Caliphate," and Ahmadi counter-charged that Perez was "contaminated by an evident and odious bias toward true Islam." As for the solution, Perez focused on "the latest technology of detection" and a "significant beefing up of the counter-espionage unit of the Police Department." Ahmadi focused on the merits of Islam. He described it as the religion "best equipped to clean up a world overcome by personal corruption and meaningless lives." He contrasted it to Christianity, which, "though once great, had lost its compass, demanding little and getting less from its followers." He said he could win if every Muslim of voting age would bother to vote. Early polling indicated 95 percent had pledged to.

Each had ten minutes to summarize his main points, and Silas spoke last. He wore a new gray-blue suit that Saira cajoled him into buying and that fit him perfectly. He was looking good, very good, but was as nervous as an excited schnauzer.

"Friends, there is much truth in what my colleagues are saying. Yes, we do need better technology to track down criminals, and more police will always be useful. And, yes, Islam is a great religion with much to offer the world, and in just the way that Mr. Ahmadi describes. But to say the solution is more of the right kind of Islam is of no help. He didn't tell us *how* to propagate that kind of Islam. And instead of contrasting true Islam to its poisonous perversion, he contrasted it to Christianity, as if Christianity were the problem! As my imaginative wife said, instead of eliminating the venomous rattlesnake, he eliminated the harmless garter snake.

"As you all know, I'm a member of that religion that 'has lost its compass,' as Mr. Ahmadi put it. Allow me to digress a moment. What makes Christianity unique in the world, and what attracts me to it in spite of its many flaws? Its emphasis on forgiveness—that's what the world needs above everything else. In Jesus's day people suffered terribly under the wrongs done to them, just as we do today. My friends, hatred destroys the hater, not the one you hate. That's a terrible irony, but it's true. If you hate your enemy, even if he's scammed you out of all your savings or destroyed your reputation at work, you undercut your own happiness, you contaminate it. In many parts of the world, Muslims condone honor killing, and that's hating in its worst form. The Christian could easily say—but I won't—that Islam has 'lost its compass.' The moral of this little digression is that we should be slow to find fault in our brother's religion and quick to find it in our own.

"Now, how do we, we New Yorkers, resist the evil that is all around us and that calls itself the Caliphate? We have bent over backward to accommodate their most recent demands. In several countries where Islam dominates, especially in the Arab world, any Christian who dared to ring a bell to announce a religious service would be put to death. Yet the Caliphate insists on a prayer, the salat, five times a day in our country. This salat, amplified so no one can fail to hear it, rains down on all five of our boroughs. There is no escaping it. I ask you: is that fair? Many Muslims see the arrogance of this and understand the reasons for a compromise. You all know the details—the same that my Muslim wife proposed in London four months ago; the same that became the law of the land there three weeks ago.

"How, then, should we resist the arrogance of the Caliphate? We know, after a century of suicide bombings and beheadings, that there is no quick fix. Caliphate supporters are victims of an upbringing that threatened them with eternal hell if they deviated from their ideology. And, as you know, that ideology is to conquer the world for Islam no matter how much killing is needed. It's inconceivable to them that they could be wrong. There is no reasoning with them. But if they'd been brought up differently, if they'd been taught from an early age that there are many different ways to God, they'd be spared this delusion. They wouldn't think there was only one way. They would be more modest and stop thinking that God detests Hindus and Buddhists and Sikhs, and barely tolerates Jews and Christians. And the world would be spared the violence and hatred their ideology inspires.

"The way to fight this delusion, here in our beloved Gotham, is to require a broad religious education in our schools. It should begin in the third grade and continue right on through high school. It will require that our teachers be trained to teach the basic principles and practices of the world's main religions. The purpose would not be to convert. It would be to teach our kids *about* religion, not indoctrinate them. It would introduce them to the many religious options out there in the world. It would show them that no religion—not Islam or Christianity or any other faith—has a monopoly on God's pleasure.

"If elected, I'll introduce legislation that will ensure such an outcome. A basic knowledge of the world's nine largest religions will be a graduation requirement. All of our kids will have to pass a test in order to graduate. It won't matter whether your

Kaitlyn is attending a Catholic high school or your Abdul a Muslim madrasa or your Andre one of our public schools. This test will be the same for all, and it will be crafted by a team of specialists. My doctorate at the University of Chicago was in religion, and I will personally oversee the construction of this test. I hope to see my own Izzy and Eliot take it. In addition, every kid will have to pass the written test that all immigrants seeking U.S. citizenship have to pass. This will also be a graduation requirement. This is not a difficult test, but it's a good introduction to the way our democracy works. And it's taken in English. Best of all, on passing this test, your children will gain the right to vote. They will be officially registered. So, if I am elected, your children's diploma will guarantee more than access to a better job. First, it will ensure that they understand the way our American democracy works. Second, it will give them the right to vote in our city's elections in the law-abiding, peace-loving American way. And third, it will neutralize the deadly venom of thinking that only one religion is true and all the rest are garbage. These are my promises to you. All three degrade and torpedo the goals of the Caliphate.

"So I call out to you. Christians, consider where your vote for Mr. Perez will take our city. What he offers you is a Band-aid. It doesn't attack the Caliphate problem at its root. It doesn't offer a vision for how to eradicate religious violence. At best it provides a temporary shield from the flames of hell, but it doesn't do anything to help put them out. Muslims, I am well aware that the great majority of you identify with Mr. Ahmadi and that it's only natural for you to vote for him. But ask yourselves: What has he proposed that will defeat the Caliphate? He pleads with you to distance yourself from it, and he gives reasons why you should. This is good: I strongly encourage you to do this. But is it enough? The violence continues.

"Now consider what you get with me: a Christian, but a person who understands and respects true Islam, sees its virtues, and is married to a celebrated Muslim leader. You will be hearing from her in a televised debate later this month. I confer with her on all matters dealing with religion. Her insights shine—like a diamond rotated under sunlight. We are a team.

"A final word to all you secularists who want nothing to do with God or religion. If I were to ask you to describe the God you don't believe in, it's a sure bet I'd tell you I don't believe in him either. In graduate school I escaped the cramping theology I grew up with. I found a joyous, compassionate, loving, powerful, boundless, light-filled Reality at the hub of the universe with an outreach that extended to the epicenter of my soul. This vision of God works well with the kind of Christianity I profess. This God is inclusive and has no favorites. This God delights in all well-meaning people and loves even those who make a mess of their lives. It is said that we humans become like the God we believe in. Consider this when you vote next month.

"For almost twenty years I've been writing columns for the *New York Times,* and many of them have been about the Caliphate. Some of them have earned me fatwas, three at last count. What some would call a miracle saved me from death in my apartment many years ago. My wife, Saira, is also living under a fatwa. We know that we could die at any time, but we are prepared to die, and we've prepared our children for the possible death of one of us. If I become your mayor, I will devote my life to the protection of your children as if they were my own. We have many problems to solve over the next four years, but none is so pressing as the threat to our lives from the Caliphate. If we work together, we can defeat this enemy—my enemy, your enemy, the world's enemy.

"May God bless you."

Three days before the election an ad featuring Saira, speaking alone, went viral. She wore a purple abaya with a white hijab that fit tightly around her head and ears and neck. All there was to see was a face that looked more like thirty-five than fifty-one.

She was stunning, majestic. It cost the campaign a mere $1700 to make the ad. She claimed that a team of New York's leading Muslim scholars and imams were working with her to "reorganize" Islam in America, and that they had already found a way to see Christianity as a "brother religion." She went on to say that a team of the city's leading Sunni and Shia clerics had embraced and kissed each other and sworn to take the lead in ending their worldwide 1500-year war. Finally, she described how both sides pledged to die if necessary to end the tyranny of the Caliphate. "If a woman is willing to die for this cause," they stated in a document she held up for all to see, "then how can we hold back?"

Almost before the polls had time to register the defections from Perez and Ahmadi, the election was upon them. They had misfired disastrously. It was too late.

# Chapter 25

The last seven mayors of New York City lived in Gracie Mansion with their families, but, dating back to the tenure of Michael Bloomberg in the early twenty-first century, three had decided to live in their own homes and turn the Mansion over to "the People." Thus, it had become known as "the People's House" and functioned as such when no one was living in it. During those off-years it was a popular tourist attraction. Teachers would take their classes to the Mansion, which was built in 1799 and most recently renovated in 2111, to learn about the history of their city. During the on-years, including the last forty-eight, tours were restricted to Wednesdays; and only the first floor was open to the public since the mayor's family occupied the upper.

But in February 2122 the Mansion was to be returned to the people once again. The mayor-elect, Silas Wyatt, former columnist for the *New York Times*, decided to stay put in his North Bronx home. The "good old days" would return, and the media played it up as a jubilant occasion.

There had been much discussion in the Wyatt household over the Mansion. The outgoing mayor, whose Hindu wife cooked Indian, had the upper story smelling strongly of curry when the official visit from the new mayor and his family took place. Izzy overlooked the smell and fought hard for the move, and Uncle E sided with her. But Silas was unconvinced. "Honey," he said sweetly to Izzy, "we could be in the Mansion for eight years, and you could get accustomed to it, and feel denied when you finally had to leave it. And it could give you, well, airs."

"That's ridiculous, Dad. That's not going to happen! I'd just like to live in splendor for a little while. It would be such fun!"

"You'd go to a different school, sweetie, and miss your senior year with your friends."

She became quiet and thoughtful. "Can we move in after I

graduate?"

"We could. But we won't. Don't get me wrong. I'm swept away by the beauty of the place. I love it. But I don't want to live in it. For me it would be a corrupting influence."

Saira said, "Izzy, your dad is probably the least wealthy man ever to hold this office. He has simple tastes."

Silas didn't feel Saira had put it quite right, but he left it at that.

But Izzy was not done. For her junior year history project, she got permission to do an oral history on the return of Gracie Mansion to the people. At the grand opening she would mingle among the crowd and record what she heard. Eliot was fascinated by the idea and told his parents he would go too—as a spy. "I'll report back what I hear as I walk around listening." His eyes glistened at the thought of spying.

Saira laughed and laughed, then said, "All right, you guys, your old mom will go too."

"No, Mom," said Izzy. "You'll be the center of attention and ruin it for me."

"Then I'll go incognito like you, darling. I'll wear that old niqab buried at the back of my closet. No one will know. And I'll do some interviewing of my own."

"But the guard will know, Mom."

"You're right. Hmm. Well, I'll swear him to secrecy with the help of a nice little tip. How about you, Si? Can you join us on our little safari? You could wear a powdered wig like Washington or Jefferson. It's a costume party, you know. It would be like hiding behind the bushes and hunting lions."

He laughed. "I'm afraid not. I've got six deputy mayors to appoint. I can barely remember what I was elected to do! And, Izzy, you could be recognized. Your mug appeared all over social media. You'll need a disguise."

Izzy hit upon the idea of buying an Afro and applying bronzing cream to her face. She got both online from Amazon, and they arrived by drone at their home in Spuyten Duyvil that very day. She was all set.

Speaking of that home, it came with the most advanced security system on the market once Silas was elected, and a sentry was stationed in a camper in front of the home around the clock. In the middle of the lawn in the backyard Silas had planted a cherry tree to commemorate his trip to Japan and friendship with Toshihiro Shima. It broke his heart to see it removed to make space for the flyaway that would take him to work at City Hall downtown. It was in that flyaway, with seats for four, that the family left for Manhattan on a brisk Saturday morning to attend the grand opening of the home they might have had. Saira had a hard time closing the door around her niqab, and Izzy adjusted her Afro, which the wind had blown sideways on her face. They landed on the helipad atop City Hall, and the partygoers—and spy—took a short cab ride to Gracie Mansion. Like all the attendees, they had to wait in line, show identification, and be photographed for security reasons. The guard didn't show surprise when the three Wyatts presented their IDs, so Saira, somewhat puzzled, decided to kill the tip idea. They marched in, Izzy with her phone ready to take notes and photograph her interviewees if permitted, and Eliot with nothing more than his strange and remarkable mind.

Half the attendees paid good money "for the upkeep of the Mansion" to get in, while the other half came by lottery—each could bring two "guests." Some wore costumes, others normal dress. Within minutes of entering the building, it was clear the disguises had worked. The family split up, with Izzy commandeering visitors on the ground floor, and Eliot heading upstairs. Poor Saira felt out of place; she was the only one wearing a niqab or burqa; she was handsomely clothed underneath, but what did it matter? She could have been the life of the party, but instead she felt scrutinized and quietly disapproved of. She was tempted to throw off the disguise but remembered Izzy's warning.

She walked by herself all over the house, loved the curtains, the antique armoires, the chandeliers, the sculptures and paintings, the curving staircase leading upstairs, the view over the East River on this sunny, windy day. She was recently honored with a visit to the White House, but she saw nothing there to compare with the exquisite fusion of the old and the new in Gracie. It made her heart ache at the thought of giving all this up, and all she could do was sigh. She contented herself by observing Izzy and Eliot at their work.

About an hour into the visit, as she eavesdropped on Izzy interviewing, Eliot came rushing down the great staircase and pulled his mother aside. "Mom, did you see those three guys wearing those masks?"

She had. They wore patriotic masks. "What about them?"

"Mom, I heard them say something about bombing—I think they meant this building. They said they had their stuff in a car, and they were going to get it."

"What? Eliot, are you sure? Where are they now?"

"They're still upstairs."

"Show me. But don't make it seem like we're suspicious. Are you sure you didn't imagine this, like Jimmy? Eliot, this isn't a game."

"Mom, I'm a good spy. I hid behind a door and listened. They didn't know I was there."

"Okay, I'm glad you're a good spy. But let's go see anyway."

As they turned to go, the three faces walked down the stairs toward the front of the building.

Saira yanked out her phone and called 911. "Just spotted three guys wearing masks walking out of Gracie Mansion. Think they might be planning to bomb the Mansion. This is Saira Wyatt, the mayor's wife. I'm following them."

She hurried down the front stairs and reached the guard. "Did you see three men just now exit the building? They wore masks—Obama, MLK, Lincoln, I think!"

"No, ma'am."

She craned her head and looked up and down East End Avenue. She couldn't see them.

A police cruiser pulled up just then, and she ran up to it. "I called in the 911 just now. Three men wearing masks, but they might have removed them. My son said he overheard them talking about blowing up the building. But I don't see them."

"Are you the mayor's wife?" said a sergeant whose badge read *Kim.*

"Yes. My son said they might be going to a car to get explosives. This is urgent."

"Where is he? We need to speak to him."

She looked around. "He's only seven. Maybe back in the building. No, wait. I think I saw him go out ahead of me. Knowing him, he might be trying to follow them. He's wearing a gray cap."

A swarm of cruisers drove up, all with sirens muted. Police jumped out and consulted. Sergeant Kim said, "Look for a kid about seven. Brett, you go north on East End; Hector, you go south." As more officers arrived, he dispatched them down East 86th to 90th Streets as far as York Avenue. "Look for a seven-year-old boy with a gray cap," he said. "He might know where the suspects are—three guys, maybe wearing patriotic masks. If you find them, arrest them on the spot. If they resist, block off the street. They might be extremely dangerous. Maybe wearing suicide vests. Carla, go inside the building. The kid might still be in there. Ask him what he heard. This could all be a false alarm. It all comes from the boy."

Three minutes later the officer on 88th Street called in. "Sheila here. We have the boy. Recommend we close street from East End to York immediately. Suspects in pod a hundred yards ahead. Maroon Ford. Boy sticks by his story. Await instructions."

Before Sergeant Kim could reply, Saira said, "I'm going with you."

He said, "Just a minute. Yes. We're sealing 88th between East End and York. Disable their vehicle. Repeat: Use your disabler on their vehicle. I'll be there in less than a minute."

"I think they see us," Sheila said.

"Wait for me. Don't do anything until I get there. Oh, did the kid see inside the vehicle?"

A pause. "He says no. He just heard them talk about blowing up the Mansion. And he followed them here."

"Any masks?"

There was another pause. "The kid says they took them off. They should be on the lawn back at the Mansion. By the front steps, he says."

"All right. We're definitely going to treat this as the real thing." Kim's cruiser zoomed up beside Sheila's. Kim reached for the broadcaster and amplified the sound. "All of you in the maroon Ford. This is the police. Come out with your hands up. Come out into the middle of the street."

"Mom! Mom!" came a voice from the cruiser parked on the curb beside them.

"Sergeant Kim, can my son join us?"

"Yes, but make it quick."

"Mom," said Eliot as he jumped in beside her on the back seat. "Those are real bad guys."

Kim turned back and said, "I'll have Sheila take you and your son back to—"

"Not on your life!" said Saira. "We've got skin in this game. And I think I know how to talk to the suspects better than you boys, no disrespect intended."

Kim was quiet. Then he repeated over the broadcaster, "This is the police. Come out with your hands up. Out into the middle of the street."

Nothing but silence…

"Sergeant, give me the broadcaster," said Saira.

"This is against the rules, ma'am. I'm sorry—"

"I'll answer to the authorities," she said. "The broadcaster, please!"

He handed it back and she called out. "Brothers, I am a Muslim. My name is Saira Wyatt. I am the new mayor's wife. You might know me. You are about to harm innocent people. Some of them will be Muslim. Don't do this. Come out and show Allah what you are: men of compassion and mercy, true followers of Muhammad, blessed be his name. Whoever put you up to this is misguided."

Police were entering the buildings on both sides of East 88th where the car was parked. People were curious to know what was going on. "Get all those people away from the windows!" radioed a captain, who was taking over control from Kim.

Meanwhile there was no response from the Ford.

"Mom, I think Dad would be proud of me," said Eliot.

"Yes, he would," said Saira. "Any ideas about what to say to the bombers?" She was serious. Words of uncanny wisdom would sometimes slip out of little Eliot's mouth. Even when Jimmy wasn't there.

"Tell them God wants them to have kids and bring little Muslims into the world," he said.

Eliot's words dislodged in Saira a memory of something Silas wrote a long time ago. "Friends of the Prophet," she called over the broadcaster. "A long life with children and grandchildren to hang on your neck and kiss your cheeks is what Allah wants for you. It is not to be given up lightly."

From a cruiser at the other end of the street, the captain's voice rang out: "That was the mayor's wife speaking. I have a different message: You have not yet committed a serious crime. We will go easy on you if you give yourself up. Consider the options and choose like a true disciple of Islam."

"No!" said Saira to Sergeant Kim. "That is not the right message. That could lead to—"

At that moment the door of the Ford opened and a man

dashed away from the Ford with his hands up. His exit was followed by a huge explosion and fireball that engulfed the Ford and swallowed up the fleeing man. Saira and Eliot felt a gust of heat penetrate the closed windows of their cruiser, then dissipate. All around were small pockets of fire. The fleeing man was one of them.

Mother and son stared at each other for an instant as Kim called for ambulances and fire trucks. Then Eliot opened the door and stepped out and began approaching the burning man.

"Eliot, what are you doing!?" yelled Saira, who jumped out of the cruiser to bring him back. But Kim was quicker. He caught up with Eliot and lifted him off his feet.

"What are you doing, little man?" he said. They ran back to the safety of the cruiser.

Then came a command from the captain, "Sergeant Kim, use your fire extinguisher to save the man. Everybody else stay put. There might be more explosives. And for God's sake keep the kid in the cruiser!"

It all happened so fast that it left Saira dazed. The burning man barely survived—his winter clothing saved him—but the other two were mangled and fried beyond recognition. Eliot was fascinated by what he'd seen and told his mother on the way home he would join the CIA when he was big. Izzy interviewed thirty-one people up until the explosion, when all the guests were evacuated from the Mansion and dogs were brought in to sniff for any possible explosives. "Most of them loved what Dad did," she later reported, "but more Christians voted for Perez than for Dad. Dad scored big with the Muslims, and of course he got all the seculars. A few said they voted for him as the least of all the evils. One woman said he looked like an owl, but a nice owl." Saira was still too numb to laugh.

Within hours the news around the world celebrated the kid who prevented a catastrophe. On Monday Eliot's school was besieged by paparazzi, and Eliot made his entrance into the school yard between cameras flashing. His classmates, who had always thought him strange since he made the mistake of telling them about Jimmy, showed new respect and clustered around him. Silas had to put an end to calls for details from the media.

Silas was, of course, overjoyed that Eliot uncovered the plot by his stealth, but a detail that was missed by everyone else was not missed by him. The man who narrowly escaped death turned out to be Nadheer, the humble Yemeni who came to kill him seventeen years ago. *What an extraordinary coincidence,* he thought. After his second prison visit years ago, Silas thought he had converted Nadheer to a gentler expression of Islam, or even to Christianity. He left Nadheer in tears when he mentioned the money he sent his wife. And now this.

A week after the incident, Silas visited the Harlem Burn Center. It wasn't to offer condolences to Nadheer, but to try to understand what drove him once again to murder. Reporters had tried to gain access to him, but his condition was too critical to allow visitors except for his wife. No one knew why he fled the vehicle before the explosion, and it was this that Silas was most curious about. The attending doctor allowed him the visit.

Silas found Nadheer hooked up to IV tubes and his disfigured, hairless face barely recognizable. He was awake but didn't seem at first to recognize the presence of a visitor.

"Nadheer," said the nurse who accompanied Silas into the room, "you have a visitor. He says he is an old friend. I'll leave the two of you together. Buzz at any time." She closed the door behind her.

"Nadheer, do you recognize me?"

Nadheer studied the visitor, then began sobbing.

"It's all right. It's like the first time we met. Do you remember? You came to kill me. Do you remember?"

The voice that eventually answered was feeble and slow. "Yes, you are the mayor. What are you doing here visiting this miserable soul?"

"Do you feel up to talking?"

"There's nothing else to do."

"Nadheer, you are not very good at killing. There is a purity in you. You are not a miserable soul."

Nadheer thought for a moment and said, "I'm a failure at everything. I didn't even kill myself. This is my punishment."

"The others are dead. You are alive."

"They are in Paradise. What am I?"

"Nadheer, can you tell me why you left the pod before it blew up?"

He was quiet for a long time, and Silas thought he had lost him. But he came to and said, "It was the woman—what she said. I thought about my kids and grandkids. I knew I couldn't carry it through. But when that policeman spoke, threatening us, my friends cried out, 'Allahu Akbar.' I knew what that meant and tried to get away. I wasn't fast enough."

"You were fast enough to save your life and see your kids and grandkids. Nadheer, that's no small thing."

There was a pause, then, "I guess not." There was another pause, then, "I want to thank you for the gifts you sent my wife."

Another pause. "Nadheer, I thought you agreed never to turn again to violence. Do you remember my last visit? Maybe five years ago?"

"I remember."

"What made you change your mind?"

The nurse poked her head in and asked, "How's he doing?"

"Very well, considering," said Silas. He turned back to Nadheer and asked, "Are you in pain?" The nurse closed the door.

"Yes."

"Can you tell me why you changed your mind?"

Another long pause. "Fifteen years. When I got out of prison, I couldn't get a decent job, except with the Caliphate. They treated me like a brother, and, well, I came again to believe in their mission."

"Do you believe in it now?"

No response.

"Nadheer, can you tell me? Do you believe in it now?"

"I don't know."

"Nadheer. Twice you changed your mind at the last minute. You were not born to kill. You have a pure heart, like all good Muslims."

"I guess."

"It is so. Take heart. Your wife and kids are waiting for you. She tells me your oldest son will be graduating from high school in June. You must be there. And I'll be there with you if you invite me." A pause. "Will you remember to invite me?"

Nadheer began to sob again and couldn't stop. Silas bent down and kissed him ever so gently on his charred leathery gray cheeks. He remembered how he did that the first time they parted, when the gesture had been a trick. This time it was not a trick.

# Chapter 26

On a sunny, cool Sunday in early September of 2122, less than a year after the election, Ethan turned eighty-six. Maddy, whose love for her old husband could never be described as ardent, decided to surprise him with a small birthday party. The only guests were to be the Wyatts. "And the highlight of the party will be a game of Monopoly," she told Saira over the phone. "I've booked the flyover to reach your house at four if that's okay. Ethan turns in early nowadays."

They boarded Uncle E's "beast" (named because it was a six-seater) in the middle of the street between their house and the guard's camper and flew east of the city over to Ethan's Greenwich home. Nine minutes later they touched down on an asphalt surface surrounded by hydrangeas in full bloom and climbed out. The old man lurched out of the house with cane in hand and a great welcoming smile on his creased face. Maddy would have preferred it otherwise, but there was no doubt that Silas and his family were his best friends.

They enjoyed a tri-tip cooked on site by a chef hired especially for the occasion. The Wyatts rarely ate beef, but when it showed up, they loved it. They sat around a table on the deck; it overlooked dozens of sailboats anchored in the cove below. Ice cream and cake topped off the meal, and the game of Monopoly was to come next, but was to be played inside because it was getting chilly.

As they sat down to play, and Ethan was dealing out $1500 to each of the participants, he announced, "There are five of you and only one of me, but I'll beat all of you four out of five times." He had a roguish smile on his face, and you could almost imagine him licking his chops.

"No way, E, it's too much a game of chance," said Silas.

But as the game progressed, and Ethan made his moves, usually trading expensive properties for cheaper, his foes gradually went bankrupt. Finally, only Silas and Ethan were left, but five minutes later, when Silas landed on a hotel on St. James Place, Ethan triumphed. He smiled and said, "See? I told you so."

Both men noted how Eliot stuck around the table and watched the game progress even though he had been eliminated first. Izzy was next, and she was content to settle down on a sofa and catch up on her texts. When the women bowed out, there wasn't much else for them to do but talk to each other, a conversation neither looked forward to.

Saira's one social weakness was that she disdained small talk—she called it "snappy chatter," and it bored her silly. Even worse was gossip, a vice that in her view women were especially prone to—and she was no exception—but that her religion forbade. They put on sweaters and walked out onto the boat dock stretching a few yards out over the water. After the usual dancing around possible topics of mutual interest, Maddy gave Saira an opening that engaged her.

"Do you remember the first time we went sailing? I'd just turned forty, and I wasn't very happy about it. And now, God forbid, I'm almost sixty. And it gets harder and harder to hide the wrinkles." She looked wistfully toward the west, where the sun had set and left behind a glow.

"I do remember that," said Saira. "I remember it because you told me about all those girly things you loved—lipsticks, creams, perfumes, facials, manicures, all those things that keep a woman looking good. I didn't admit I loved them too. Instead I gave you a lecture on religion. After we left, I felt like a hypocrite."

"That's not how I remember it. I remember the word *diversion,* how you said we go from one diversion to the next all day long, and how you don't need diversions if you have God in your life. I never forgot it, even though at the time I thought you were a fanatic. But you've got something I don't have."

"What's that?"

"I'm not sure. But I have followed you. I know you're famous. I know you speak out for the kind of religion I can respect. You're not a fanatic. You're...you're...I don't know." Then she said in a voice that wavered, "I'm not happy."

With that admission Saira's heart melted. She reached out for Maddy's hand and clasped it in both of hers. The glow in the west was not quite enough to reveal the tears in her eyes. Maddy began sobbing, and Saira let loose her hands and gathered her in her arms.

They stood for a moment on the dock clasped to each other. Then Saira released her and said, "You will find your way, Maddy. But you must search. If you know how to pray, that would help. And don't give up all those diversions. Just make a little time every day for the search."

Then, in a moment of stunning humility, Maddy said, "Would you help me?"

From that point on, Saira had a new friend. And one day, after one of her visits to "the mosque on the cove," as she referred in her own thoughts to the Greenwich house, Ethan told her that Maddy was a "different girl."

# Chapter 27

Midway into his third year, Silas Wyatt was widely referred to by his admirers as "the kids' mayor." From the start he fought for the acquisition of run-down properties to convert into basketball and volleyball courts. If he'd had his way, he would have followed the example of the Japanese, who managed to build baseball fields with high fences in the middle of their cities. But the cost was too high, and he settled for one "BV complex" every six square blocks.

But it was his almost manic commitment to citywide religious education that earned him the name. Ironically, the Caliphate helped build this reputation—and in a way that was unthinkable. Qadira Othman, whose grandparents brought her over from Palestine to the City when she was a baby, had grown to be Islam's wealthiest woman, worth over $3 billion. Now in her late sixties, she had built a company from the ground up that catered to Muslim women's tastes, especially luxury items. Clothing, shoes, purses, cosmetics, perfumes—she knew her customer base and gave them everything they wanted. She was a one-company conglomerate, a Nieman Marcus, Gucci, Chanel, Christian Dior, and Louis Vuitton wrapped into a single package.

Qadira loathed everything the Caliphate stood for, especially its subjugation of women. It rankled her that women were not permitted to pray alongside men in the main hall of their mosques. When women retaliated by setting up women-only mosques, with female imams, the Caliphate hit back hard with their bombs or guns. No sooner had a building been converted into such a mosque than it had to close for repairs. The persecution was relentless.

Qadira—everyone called her by her first name—found a way she thought would vanquish the threat. The old Trump Tower building in midtown Manhattan, renamed the Khadijah

Center, had become a gathering place for New York's Muslims. The building's condominiums, which took up most of its sixty stories, were rundown by the City's exacting standards and failed to attract New York's finest, as it once did. But the immense street-level atrium was as beautiful as ever, and Muslims were happy to adopt it and make it their own. The three-story penthouse where the Trumps had once lived in splendor also retained much of its stature, but it had remained on the market for years without a buyer—mostly because the building was regarded as "too Muslim."

Qadira figured that if she bought the penthouse, no one could reach and vandalize it. The building was well guarded, and she could pay to station a guard around the clock at the elevator entrance dedicated to bypass all floors except the penthouse—just in case. She thought of it as "my Titanic without the iceberg." The owner was happy to sell it to someone at last, and Qadira figured that $22 million was a steal. It took five months to convert the penthouse into a mosque, certainly the finest women-only mosque the world had ever seen.

For six weeks women gathered on Fridays at noon, heard a sermon from one of the mosque's three female imams, and worshipped in place on the rich carpets that covered the main floor and balcony. The bright colors of the rainbow, from the decorative paintings on the walls to the fashionable abayas worn by the women, "came close to rivaling the splendors of paradise," enthused one of the worshippers in her blog. The women put on a fashion show for the Lord. After the worship they typically mingled and chatted and looked out of the windows at the city's buildings, or the ocean beyond the Battery, or Central Park with the colors of the season. It was hard to imagine how paradise could be much better, except that the Lord would be present.

On a late September Friday in 2125 shortly after noon, five men dressed in black jeans and gray shirts forced at gunpoint the driver of a black flyaway limousine to fly up next to the penthouse and "park." The women barely noticed the low hum of the vehicle's engine through the drawn curtains and concentrated on the sermon, which had just begun. At a signal the windows of the limousine opened, and four of the men aimed cut-off automatic rifles out of the side windows of the car while the fifth dug his pistol into the neck of the driver. They yelled together "Allahu Akbar!" and opened fire through the windows. Twenty-seven women died. Seventy-three were wounded.

The tragedy shocked the world and cut deeply into the morale of the women, including Qadira. The stock market plunged, but this time anger was not turned toward Islam, since Muslims were the victims. Non-Muslims saw more clearly than ever that there were two Islams, and that "the good one" was their friend and ally against a common enemy. Silas declared a day of mourning, and after a week passed, the mood of the city changed. Recognizing this, he realized that it was time to act. What had been a rugged battle for religious education suddenly found wide support. Even highly conservative Muslims, who had been skeptical of any outside intrusion of religion into their private schools, were signing on. More than that, they became the most vocal body of support for the idea. Letters from Muslims flooded the media at an unprecedented level. And Saira organized a march from City Hall to the Tower and supported her husband's plan. The upshot of this indignation and outrage was that the Department of Education, at Silas's impassioned urging, mandated religious education for seventh and eighth graders at all public and private schools within the five boroughs. More than that, he won support for a "Religion Bee" at the end of the eighth grade, with the top students vying for a city championship. In the thousands of city schools, students would compete for the honor of representing their school, then their district, then their region, right up the line. That was his idea. The finals would be held at the refurbished Town Hall on West 43rd Street—he had already worked out a contract. By then the contestants would be whittled down to eight: four from the city's public schools, one from a Jewish school, one from a Catholic school, one from an Islamic school, and one from a charter or other school not represented, with none left out.

Every time Silas was challenged over the wisdom of spending $50 million on textbooks and retooling the city's teachers for their new task, he would say there would be no more Khadijahs. "The kids will end up teaching their parents and grandparents. It will take time, but it will work. You'll see."

The tragedy had one other effect. It catapulted him into a second term as mayor.

# Chapter 28

On June 1, 2127, a queue of school buses in front of Town Hall unloaded students and teachers from eight schools eager to cheer their champions on. Parents, relatives, friends, the media, the governor of New York and his staff, members of the Department of Education and the mayor's office, and representatives from school districts all over the country claimed their places in the 1500-seat auditorium. Silas, who was backstage with the contestants, realized he could have rented Madison Square Garden and filled it. He glowed.

He insisted that Esther Assante, head of City Education, introduce the contestants and explain the rules. He took his place next to Saira as an anonymous viewer in the fifth row.

Professors Clay Townsend of Fordham, Liora Goodblatt of Jewish Theological Seminary, and Silas's dear old friend Layla Haddad took turns asking the questions. Silas had been concerned that members of the audience might spontaneously call out answers to the questions and had sound absorbers installed. Onstage all one could hear from the crowd was a low, indistinct drone.

Ms. Assante told the audience that the students were responsible for questions on nine religions: Judaism, Christianity, Islam, Hinduism, Buddhism, Sikhism, Spiritualism, Bahai, and Native American religion; and that several of the religions included different sects: for example, Mormonism would fall under Christianity, Sunni and Shia Islam would be lumped together, and Brazilian Spiritism would fall under Spiritualism. She offered apologies to anyone who might find these groupings misleading or offensive.

The questions were designed to grow in difficulty as the program progressed.

Professor Goodblatt: "This question is for Jaylen Davis, from

Jesse Owens School in Brooklyn. This religion, the youngest of the nine you've studied, places great emphasis on humanity as one global family and the earth as one homeland."

Jaylen, an African American, answered: "Bahai."

Goodblatt: "Correct."

Professor Townsend: "This question is for Zimal Mostafa, from Al-Mamoor Islamic School, Queens. Zimal, this religion gives the Divine many names and personalities and delights in picturing them."

Zimal, a tiny girl of Egyptian background: "Hinduism."

Townsend: "Excellent."

Professor Haddad: "This question is for Robert Wu, from Horace Mann School in the Bronx: This religion worships God through a book, which it calls its Guru."

Robert, a boy of mixed races: "Sikhism."

Haddad: "Correct. Thank you, Robert."

As hoped, the students found the basic questions easy pickings, and there were no stumbles. Silas whispered to Saira, "Thank God the questions were drawn clearly enough."

"Yeah, there's so much overlapping at the basic level...She looks good, doesn't she?"

"Who? You mean Layla?"

"Yeah."

"She's done well for herself. The move to IUNY was really something. Dean of Religious Education at the biggest Islamic university in the country—"

"I mean the way she looks."

"Oh, yeah, she does look good. Not as good as you, though." There was a tiny bat squeak of jealousy in Saira's remark, and Silas picked up on it right away. He was always careful to downplay his attachment to Layla when her name came up.

As the program progressed, the questions got more arcane, and students began to miss. Jessica Quackenbush, a white girl from Catholic Convent of the Sacred Heart in Manhattan, couldn't remember the Western equivalent of the first year of the Islamic calendar. And Yusri Abbasi, a husky boy of Syrian background from The Christa McAuliffe School in Manhattan, couldn't recall the name of the pope who convened the Third Vatican Council.

In the end it came down to a tie between Tamra Beloff, a Jewish girl from the Kinneret Day School in the Bronx, and Gabriel Martinez, a kid of Mexican heritage from the Amber Charter School in Manhattan. They were the only ones who hadn't missed a question.

The audience watched in amazement as boy and girl answered correctly one esoteric question after another. But it had to end sometime. And it did when Tamra correctly matched the Tibetan Buddhist bodhisattva Chenrezig with the Goddess of Mercy, and Gabriel could not name the sage Hillel as the author of the famous Jewish saying: "That which is hateful to you, do not do to your fellow. That is the whole Torah; the rest is commentary; go and learn."

The event roused the media. News sources all over the world acclaimed its importance. The *Times of India* rejoiced that no one seemed to object to placing Islam and Hinduism side by side as equals, and *Al Jazeera* hailed it as "the road to world peace." Even the partisan Council on American Islamic Relations gave it tepid praise.

# Chapter 29

"Come to me, all you who are weary and weighed down, and I will give you rest." Silas thought of these words, spoken by Jesus, as he tried to fall asleep four months after the Bee. His popularity had risen to an all-time high, with his approval rate standing at 76 percent. But the thought of three more years as mayor wearied him and weighed him down.

"Can't sleep?" Saira said.

"No. I've been thinking. The truth is I'm a one-trick pony, Saira. I don't much care about the city water rates or the Bronx zoning laws or the bidding wars over the Staten Island Bridge."

"Do you take pleasure in being considered for the Nobel Peace Prize?"

He thought about it. "Yes. Because I'd be getting it for something really worth doing, something I'm proud of. Anyway, you deserve it more than me."

She snuggled up against him. "You've never excused yourself because you were bored or too tired. You've always been the servant, and those zoning laws mean a lot to people in the Bronx. Their concern is not below you. But you do need a rest. A long rest. A vacation. By yourself. Can you take a few days off?"

He was no card-carrying Catholic. Like many of the Christians who studied with him at Chicago, he came out of the experience convinced that Jesus was a charismatic Jewish reformer whose followers divinized him as their savior. The dogmas that followed in the fourth and fifth centuries, as he told Cardinal Nolan, struck him as Christian mythology. In a way he regretted his elite education, for it separated him from the common people he loved and did his best to serve. His last book had cost him more than a few friends.

He researched monasteries that made room for wayfarers like himself and found one that looked promising in Spencer,

Massachusetts. The stone buildings, colonnaded walkways, and groomed mid-summer grounds of St. Joseph's Abbey called out to him to come. Even though formal weekend retreats had to be booked more than a year in advance, he was welcome to show up midweek in any season and do his own thing. He drove his own car to the small central Massachusetts town and up to the monastery.

When the monks discovered who he was, they couldn't help being a little dazzled, but he made it clear he wanted no special attention. He had come to pray and receive instruction, and to enjoy the Gregorian chant and hike the trails through the fields and wooded hillsides that stretched outward from the buildings. He described himself as a spiritually needy soul. He hoped to stay three nights "if that is okay."

For the last forty years the Trappist monks at the abbey had been practicing Centering Prayer as their primary form of spiritual discipline. And it was this, more than the candlelit masses and arched stained glass windows, that attracted Silas to Spencer. Centering Prayer bypassed all the dogma that came with orthodox Catholicism. It even sidestepped theology. All one had to do was choose a holy word or phrase and repeat it quietly over and over. The word symbolized one's assent to the presence and activity of God within oneself. It shoved aside all thoughts and left only the sound of the word in its place. Silas chose the word *Abba,* the word Jesus used when calling out to his God. It meant *Father.*

He had experimented with this technique several times before, but he never persisted. The reason was that it was difficult and not immediately rewarding. This time he was determined to persist. But he knew he needed help. He asked the guest master if he could talk to a monk "of liberal mind and noted personal holiness."

Father Calhoun Porter introduced himself as "Father Cal, or just plain Cal." Silas could tell by looking at the kindly face of this stooped old man, easily in his mid-eighties, that he had been touched by God, whatever exactly that meant. They sat on chairs carried out and placed on the sun-dappled lawn under a spreading oak on a gorgeous late-September afternoon.

Father Cal began by asking him how he was doing with "the prayer."

"Not so well. I should explain right off that I'm not your usual Catholic. I think the prayer would be easier if I were."

"You might be surprised to know I read your book when it first came out, long before you went into politics."

"I *am* surprised. Well, you know me already."

"Silas, if you give me permission to use your name—and it's a good name—Silas traveled with Paul on his missionary journeys and was imprisoned and beaten. He ruffled feathers wherever he went, rather like you—so you are well named…ah, where was I? Ah, yes. The prayer. The prayer has nothing to do with creedal formulas."

"Just out of curiosity, Father, do you too have trouble with Catholic dogma, with Mary as the mother of God, with Jesus's ascension into heaven, and so on?"

A bird overhead repeated monotonously the same beautiful melody. "Do you hear that robin?" asked the old monk. "Where is Catholic dogma in the song of that bird? The prayer is like that song."

"Are you saying I can be a good Catholic without the dogma as long as I meet God in the prayer?"

"Hmm."

"Do *you* throw out the dogma?"

"Not a bit. It helps me to love him when I remember he sent his son to die for my sins. But that has nothing to do with my meeting him in the prayer. And that's what's important. Would you agree?"

"I *would* agree. So, are you saying I can approach the altar at mass tomorrow morning and receive communion without any scruples?"

"Silas, you have very good reasons for your position. You're a scholar, a Ph.D. It's not your beliefs that will separate you from God. It's your will. As I understand you, you're not rebelling against the dogmas because you get a kick out of it. And you're not playing up to Islam to make peace with it at any cost. Your studies have simply led you to different conclusions. I think Jesus would find you a lovely addition to his table, if that's what you want."

"That is what I want. That's a great relief to hear, Father. Thank you." Silas looked up through the rustling reddening leaves, a few of which floated to the ground around them. The robin continued to sing. "About the prayer. It's hard, terribly hard, for me to drown out the thoughts that keep surging up in my brain. And when I do calm them, I get the feeling I'm not really in contact with anything except my own deep self."

"This is a common complaint with a beginner," said the old priest. "The solution is to stay with it. You are a man of faith. Think of God as being like the air we breathe. We don't need to talk to it. We just quietly breathe it. But we're seldom aware we're breathing. God is like that. God is always within us, but we almost never realize it. Centering prayer helps us realize it."

"I know that, know the theory behind it, but the deep interior peace I'm looking for escapes me. It seems like I'm not going deep enough to experience God."

Father Cal looked out at the fields in the distance. "Silas, I don't see so well anymore. The doctors call it macular degeneration. It's a trial not to be able to read without a magnifier. Sometimes I wish I would die and go to heaven. Sometimes when I wake up I'm disappointed to find I'm not yet there. Because then I'd be able to read without a magnifier…Where was I?" He held his shriveled hand up against his brow and slumped in his chair. Then he raised himself and said, looking straight at Silas, "Yes, centering prayer. It's not easy meeting God, Silas. You need a magnifier. And your word is the magnifier. By the way, what is your word?"

"Abba."

"Good. It takes a while to read using a magnifier. You have to stay with the practice, stay with the word, and your experience will deepen. Nothing so precious as meeting God will come easy. And meeting God is the most precious thing there is. So be patient. But most of all, be persistent. Take it back to New York with you. It will make your heavy task lighter."

They talked for over an hour more, and Father Cal left him with a final thought he remembered from a book written a century earlier by the monk Thomas Keating, founder of the Centering Prayer movement in America: "The chief thing that separates us from God is the thought that we are separated from him."

The next morning Silas went to mass for the first time in over a year. One of the fifty-six monks, sixteen of them priests, the remainder brothers, preached the homily. "The world needs deep people who are willing to be transformed." Those words, which closed the homily, stayed with Silas as his car navigated its way back down the Connecticut Turnpike toward home. "How in the hell can I transform myself as the Mayor of New York?" he wondered. He promised himself he would spend twenty minutes every morning repeating his prayer word—that little word that was supposed to open him to the presence and activity of the God within.

# Chapter 30

Halfway through his second term, Silas, with Saira, traveled to India at that country's invitation to address the Department of School Education and Literacy. After New York City's Religion Bee, violence via terrorism dropped significantly. No one knew why the drop was so steep: 44 percent for the last six months of 2127 compared to the previous year. Indians followed the trend closely, and their media was filled with speculation as to what caused it. Whatever it was, they wanted it. India's terrorist problem was far more serious than America's.

So the government invited, practically begged, Silas to tell them how they might go about a feasibility study. Could India do on a massive scale what New York City did on one much smaller? They also hoped that Saira would accompany him, and they promised her prime television time if she would. Silas and Saira left New York on February 27 on a nonstop Air France flight.

Silas's work in New Delhi took place behind closed doors, and the media got news of it indirectly. Important though it was, the nation found it too abstract to rally around. But Saira fared much better on NDTV. For the first time she ventured into the dangerous territory of Quran interpretation. She made a distinction between the "word" of the Holy Book and its "heart." She waded into the quagmire of "scriptural evolution," telling a hundred million Hindus, Muslims, Sikhs, Christians, and Jains that all their scriptures passed through the fallible hands of men as they evolved. In particular, what finally appeared in the Quran was far from settled when Muhammad died in 632. What went into it depended on the will of men who came later, and whose memory of what the Prophet recited to them could not be ascertained with certainty. She gave examples of texts from both the Quran and the Christian New Testament that "no God worthy of the name could possibly have said." She closed her speech by making an impassioned appeal for her husband's school initiative.

The night after her speech "more than a dozen" death threats were called or tweeted in. The New Delhi police entreated her not to continue on to Mumbai, where she was scheduled to address a full house of 8,000 at the golden-domed Global Vipassana Pagoda. In typical fashion she brushed them off. The couple flew south under heavy guard.

Their trip was never meant to be a vacation, but Silas had set aside two days of "hiding" at a "hill station" in the mountains northeast of Mumbai. No one knew of their plans, and they left their hotel and hailed a bicycle rickshaw early the next morning. The rickshaw dropped them off at the nearest train station, and they were off to Matheran where they had a reservation at The Verandah in the Forest, a mansion built 250 years ago by a British army captain. Silas chose it because of its Victorian charm—and because, due to its out-of-the-way isolation from the noise of town, it was inexpensive. They both wore broad-brimmed straw hats and sunglasses to disguise themselves.

It was everything they expected and more. After the five-hour train trip, the last two on a "toy train" up the steep slopes toward Matheran, followed by a further one-mile trek to the town itself, and then another half-mile walk to the hotel, Saira threw herself on the broad four-poster bed and exclaimed, "This is fit for royalty!"

They ate lunch on a verandah looking out over low mountains of densely covered jungle, where tigers roamed at large when the British captain killed them by the hundreds for sport. Now there were only leopard, boar, deer, fox, and squadrons of raucous macaque monkeys, which patrolled Matheran's main street and romped on housetops. And there were snakes, quite a variety of them, including the venomous krait, Russell's viper, bamboo pit viper, and cobra. Killing snakes in India's forests was strictly forbidden, and their high population was proof of it. Silas teased Saira about her fear of snakes as they filled their water bottles for a hike to Charlotte Lake and Echo Point. He joked that she was so lean that the rock python, another tenant of the forest, could swallow her whole. They decided to leave their phones in the hotel safe so they wouldn't be tempted to let a call distract them from the pleasure of losing themselves in wild nature. "I'll text the kids and let them know we'll be offline for a while and not to worry," Saira said.

They set out about 2:30 and enjoyed the scenery with its bird-song and monkeys jumping from tree to tree. Clouds swooped down for a few minutes and enclosed them in mist, then floated away to allow a warm sunshine to work up a sweat. Except for the litter along the trails, the scenery was magnificent. "Look over there," Saira said. Through a tangle of bamboo and bushes she saw a crumbling old mansion. Farther along they saw old homes that had been renovated and were now occupied by the former servants of the rich white man two centuries earlier. All in all it was a fascinating trek, so fascinating that they lost track of time.

At five o'clock they decided to return to the hotel, which couldn't be more than a mile and a half away by Silas's reckoning. They turned and headed back the way they had come.

For some reason they weren't finding the hotel. There were many side trails that Silas hadn't kept track of on the way out, and now a queasy feeling in his stomach told him he wasn't sure which way to go. He reassured himself that they couldn't be far away, certainly not more than a half mile. The next turn would probably reveal the hotel. But it didn't, and now he noticed that there was nobody else on the crisscrossing trails. The sun had just set, and twilight loomed, then darkened a little more. They began to walk fast, eager to get to some sort of habitation if not their hotel. But the trails seemed to go nowhere, and at the next junction Silas panicked. But he kept it to himself. "I think that's the way; it seems familiar." But he really wasn't sure. He just hoped to God he made the right turn. Then he reached a place he was sure they had arrived at a half hour before. They had gone around in a circle.

They turned back the way they had come and walked faster than ever. They took a turn opposite the one they had taken earlier. Now it was almost completely dark, and he looked up and saw stars. It grew harder and harder to distinguish the trail from the forest surrounding them. He shivered as he thought of the snakes he had joked about—snakes that one of them might step on any minute. He thought of the irony of dying by snakebite instead of by a terrorist's bomb. He thought of his children motherless or fatherless. He felt an immense shame at the thought that he had brought this upon them by sheer carelessness. Shame turned into horror as he realized what they now had to do. Saira had not voiced a word of complaint; she must have realized the panic he was in and didn't want to add to it. Bless her! But now he heard her sniffling. Other than that there was not a sound to be heard in the entire dark jungle.

Trying to sound brave, he said, "Darling, we are going to have an experience that will be hard to endure. I'm afraid we're lost. It makes no sense to keep going. And it would be dangerous."

"What? Si, what are we...what are we...what are we going to do? Si, how could you...could you have let...this happen?" He could tell by her speech that she was shivering. And not from fear alone, for it was chilly.

"We're going to sit right where we are and wait for daylight, right in the middle of the trail, no, off to the side a little, but not in the bushes. We're going to keep each other warm by holding each other tight, very tight. All night long. And we're going to tell each other stories. Here, sit on your pack."

She sat down, and he sat down behind her and wrapped his legs and arms around her. They almost squeezed themselves into a single organism.

She stopped shivering and said, "I'm glad there aren't any more tigers."

"Me too."

"So we're just going to sit here?"

"That's right. Too bad we didn't bring our phones. They'd find us in a minute."

"Yeah. What about the snakes?"

"We'll just keep still."

"Get a stick, Si."

"A stick? What for?"

"To knock away a snake."

"What a strange idea." But he got up anyway in search of a stick. He came back after a minute and reported, "Too dark to see. We'll have to do without your stick."

"What if a snake sneaks up into my lap?"

"Keep extra still."

"That's not funny."

The forest was quiet, and the stars overhead gave it a personality that seemed to say these intruders were almost welcome. Time passed, and Saira's head tipped forward.

After an hour or so, Silas' position was becoming unbearable, and he gently disentangled himself from Saira and lay her back on the chilly ground next to him.

"I fell asleep, didn't I?" she said.

"You did."

"Can you sleep?"

"Not a chance."

They clung to each other as the earth pressed against their undersides and the galaxy above them turned in the night. It was hard to say which was worse: the cold earth they lay on or the chilly air on top of them.

After a long silence she said, "Did I ever tell you about my first boyfriend?"

"You had a boyfriend? What a charming thought. You never

told me."

"I met him when I was nineteen and he was eighteen, a year into my marriage."

"You had a boyfriend *after* marriage? This is getting better all the time."

"Actually I'm exaggerating a little. He wasn't really a boyfriend. He was a cashier at the neighborhood grocery store."

"Okay."

"His name was Dylan. He was cute and playful, totally unlike any Muslim boy I'd met. He kidded me about my niqab and dared me to take it off. One day I did. He was on break, and we were in the back of the store."

"This is getting better all the time. What came of that?"

"I let him kiss me. It scared me how I felt, even though I had a regular dress underneath. I ended it before it went any further. When the story broke about my adventures in the Sudan, he somehow linked me to the young married woman in the niqab."

"So, what happened?"

"I met him at a restaurant."

"You *did*?"

"I did. I was curious."

"Was he still cute?"

"He was. He was a computer programmer for IBM."

"Did you ever see him again?"

"No. But he did proposition me."

"You're kidding. Were you—were you tempted?"

"I was shocked, because actually I was, just a tiny bit. Mainly I was just flattered."

"Flattered? Why? Don't you realize ninety-nine out of a hundred men would find you attractive?"

"I guess so. But no one had ever come across to me so directly. He left no doubts about his intentions."

"So how did it end?"

"I called him a naughty boy. And then after a few more minutes I got up and left."

"That's a little scary. I never knew I had any competition!"

"It's good for you to know you do, my darling husband."

They were quiet again and listened to the dark silence. Time passed at a dreadfully slow pace. At some point the moon rose, and little slivers of light penetrated the forest here and there.

"What's that?" Saira said, sitting up suddenly.

Silas bolted up and clutched her. "My God. Shhh." There was the sound of feet thudding down on earth. There was something coming down the trail from the left, now very near and slowing down. "Be quiet, don't move," he whispered.

An animal they could faintly make out strode up to them and stopped. It sniffed audibly. It didn't move, and continued sniffing. Its eyes turned left, then right, as if considering what it would do. Then it walked on by.

"Si, what was *that*?"

"Holy crap, it was a panther! Did you see those yellow eyes?"

"I did. And I've never said such a ferocious prayer in all my life."

"What did you pray?"

"I prayed to God to protect us for our children's sake. Did you pray?"

"I did. I sent out friendly thoughts to the beast and asked him to move along."

"Apparently one of our prayers worked. I wonder which one."

He laughed, and then she did too. Then all their fear was released, and they exploded in laughter so long and loud that they forgot about the snakes and the dark night and the bombs going off all over the world.

"We're so lucky to be alive, Si," she said. "If we survive the night, it'll be one of the greatest nights of our lives."

"We'll survive. Daylight can't be too far away." He realized he was still squeezing her and let her go. They sat beside each other with their arms wrapped around their gathered legs for warmth and began another wait. Then something prompted him to confess a sin that had long troubled him.

"Saira, your story of that man moves me to a somewhat similar confession."

"Really? I'm all ears."

"This goes back to my *Times* days. Remember when I gave the commencement address at Vanderbilt?"

"Yes, that was before Eliot was born."

"Actually, it was a few months after. Anyway, there was the usual party following, and you know how I hold my liquor. One of the professors drove me over to the hotel. She walked me into the lobby and claimed she was a great fan of my writing and used my essays in class. She was a creative writing teacher, if I recall. We had drinks, and I got a little woozy—but feeling-good woozy. Darling, I slept with that woman, to my everlasting shame. It never happened again, and it never will. I've held this in for a long time and thought I'd die before telling you. But I never felt good about keeping the secret. And, besides, when we meet in the next world, it will have to come out. Better to come out now on the floor of an Indian jungle with the moon as witness. Can you forgive me?"

Saira said nothing for a few minutes, and Silas was beginning to regret what he'd done. He'd put their lives in danger; had he now wrecked their marriage too?

"Silas," she said, using his full name for the first time since their last fight six months before. "I do forgive you. It happened a long time ago, and I believe you when you say you'll never do it again. But I want you to feel my hurt. What you did is no small thing. We have a name for it: adultery. I can't take it lightly. I'm sorry, but I can't. You should atone in some way. I am asking you to give something up that you treasure, or do something out of the ordinary that costs you big. Not something for me—this is not a selfish request. But something that will help you—remember. Help you atone."

Silas kept silent for a few minutes. He was surprised at her response, which he assumed would be more forgiving. After all, it was such a long time ago, and he had resisted numerous come-ons since then, especially since he became mayor. "All right," he said. "I'll donate ten percent of my stock account to Oxfam—a lump sum. That will cost."

"No, that's too easy, and, besides, that's money put away for the children."

"Then you make a suggestion."

She said nothing for a few minutes. Then, "You will move the family into Gracie Mansion for the rest of your term."

He was taken aback and almost sputtered. "Saira, that is asking the wrong thing. My refusal to move there has opened it up to the public. You'd be taking it away from a thousand school-children who troop through the building every year."

"They won't be less for it. There are many other buildings they can visit instead. I chose this because I knew how hard it would be for you. And besides, Izzy has never quite forgiven you for staying put in our home. She won't be harmed living in splendor for two years. She's far too smart to assume it'll be the norm. You don't credit her enough. You never have."

He found the last comment infuriating but controlled himself. "Okay, we'll move," he said tersely.

"You're such a monk inside, Si. When we get there, I hope you'll allow yourself to enjoy it."

"I'll try."

"And it'll be safer. We're so exposed to terrorism in our house. We should sell our house and move into a nicer, safer one when your term is up."

They waited some more in the darkness until a faint light began to penetrate the forest. By then Silas had grown less re-sentful of Saira's demand. He didn't like what she did and liked even less what it said about her character. But he was getting used to it, and he knew he could live with it. But he had to know one thing more. "Saira, if I hadn't made this confession, would you have gotten round to making this demand anyway on some other pretext?"

"No, it wouldn't have occurred to me. I was prepared to live in Spuyten Duyvil for the rest of my life." He found her answer deeply reassuring. It was consistent with the character he had always admired. His love for her surged back into his heart, and he said, "I think I'll enjoy the Mansion too."

They had just gotten up and were preparing to resume their search when a forest ranger walked up. "Did you spend the night out here?" he asked incredulously.

"We got lost," Silas said. "We couldn't find our hotel. Can you tell us how to get to The Verandah in the Forest?"

"My God, I'll take you there!" He led them through one trail after another, a total distance of no more than half a mile. "Get yourselves cleaned up," he said. "They'll be serving breakfast any minute now. Oh, did you happen to see any game last night?"

"Actually we did. A panther."

"A panther!"

"Yes," said Saira. "It walked right up to us and stared at us with its gleaming yellow eyes, then kept going."

"Oh, you have been blessed by the gods! A panther! Imagine that. I haven't seen one for more than two years. Only signs of one. Oh, you've made my day! Thank you, sir. Thank you, madame." And he bowed to them as if they were royalty.

"Well," said Saira, as they ate breakfast sitting on the verandah looking out over the sunny forest that no longer threatened death, "you aren't a one-trick pony after all. You spot game with the best of them." And she laughed at her own joke.

# Chapter 31

Eight months after he left office, Silas Wyatt, the "kids' mayor" of New York City, received what his wife called "the world's highest honor." She was co-honoree, but she insisted it was for his work that the award was given. He disagreed. "We are a team," he said. "The Committee was under no obligation to honor you. And history tells against it." In fact, it was the first time in the long history of the Peace Prize that it had been awarded to husband and wife together.

On a snowy day in December, trumpets announced the entry of Silas and Saira into the magnificent interior of Oslo City Hall. Presidents and prime ministers from around the world, former winners of the prize, and invited guests rose as one body when the latest honorees walked through the crowd to the stage. Silas and Saira took their seats alongside five members of the Nobel Committee. As Norwegian workers from the twentieth century, painted by Sorensen in giant fresco-style mosaics on the walls of the cavernous hall, stared down at them, Silas whispered to Saira, "This can't be happening." And Saira whispered back, "I know. But it is." Last to enter were members of the Norwegian royal family, who took their seats on the front row and studied the new recipients. What they saw was an uncommonly beautiful woman wearing a beige scarf loosely covering her head over a sleek navy blue abaya reaching down to her shoe tops, and next to her a husband wearing the same gray-blue suit he wore nine years before when he made the speech that swept him into history.

The leader of the Nobel Committee, Gerda Christensen, summarized the achievements of the recipients for the first thirty-five minutes, then gave way to Silas. Preferring his notes to the teleprompter, he began:

"Friends of peace, it is with the profoundest sense of humility that I address you on this day. I am especially honored to see the heads of state of six Muslim-majority countries—Malaysia, Indonesia, Turkey, Jordan, Egypt, and Pakistan. And seated next to the Pakistani prime minister—by request, I am told—is the President of India. If this were America, we would honor Prime Minister Malik and President Subramanian with a twenty-one-gun salute. May the world take note!

"Friends of peace, Gerda Christensen generously attributed the success of the Religion Bee, both in America and especially in India, to me, but I had little to do with the startup of the Bees in other countries, significantly in Egypt and Jordan. Yes, it is true that the world has witnessed a remarkable decrease in terrorism since our children became our teachers. Even Brussels has seen high-ranking officers defect as one Arab nation after another renounces the Caliphate and withdraws its support. We are winning this war, but we still have far to go—as we saw just four days ago in the Trondheim Fjord attack on a Norwegian cruise ship. And as we saw in the Khadijah atrocity in my own city not too many months ago."

Silas went on to explain the psychology behind Islam's shift toward greater tolerance of the world's other religions. Children have a way, he said, of making complex problems and long-standing grievances seem silly and their solutions obvious. In their innocence they have a way, he continued, of shaming their parents and grandparents into better behavior.

Toward the end of his speech he emphasized the need for "a new openness" in the realm of the sacred.

"To this very day many Christians think that Adam and Eve were real people, and many Muslims think that suicide bombers go to paradise at death and consort with virgins. This wouldn't be so bad if the victims of a faulty childhood education didn't fear and hate those who were raised to believe other things. But too often they do. So you can see why I place so much emphasis on diversity in our children's religious education. It seems to be our best hope, and maybe our only hope.

"But let us not suppose that Islam is the only religion stuck in the old ways. In spite of much recent progress, Roman Catholicism, my own tradition, needs to do much more. Its central ritual, the mass, is the reenactment of the Lord's Last Supper. Why not create new rituals? Jesus's life is rich with events that Christians could model themselves after. Why not create a second mass that reenacts his great Sermon on the Mount, "the Sermon Mass"; or a third that brings to life his three or four greatest parables, "the Parable Mass"; or a fourth celebrating his seven last words before he died, "the Death Mass"? But most Christians will find such proposals frightening, unorthodox, or sacrilegious. And what we're left with is the same old mass that grows wearisome from repetition and bores young people.

"Diversity, discovery, creativity, revision, renewal: these virtues should make religion sparkle with newness and discourage dullness and the perception that there is only one way to do things. I am not suggesting a disregard for history and tradition; but these traits must be allowed to blossom under a new sun."

Silas closed his talk by turning to a subject dear to his heart since he was an undergraduate at the University of Wisconsin: the bleakness of life without the expectation of an afterlife. It was as if he were overlooking the world at large and addressing only the prize's host city:

"...Brothers and sisters of Oslo, have you forgotten that your city's highest honor is the St. Hallvard Medal? I imagine that this eleventh-century martyr, Oslo's patron saint, met his death with hope and even joy. He was held aloft by his faith in the world to come. His heroic deed is the subject of Alf Rolfsen's beautiful mosaic on the western wall of this very building.

"There is much evidence owing nothing to religion that points to our survival of death. This is very good news, especially for nonreligious people who are aging and losing their health and dread the thought of personal extinction. And it is very good news for the world at large, for this evidence makes no mention of a deity who plays favorites or sends people to hell for believing the wrong thing. It helps dispel the melancholy most of us feel at the thought of dying. It instills the confident hope that we'll make contact with those we lost to death. And it builds confidence in a divine source of immense proportions at the helm of a soul-making process stretching out over eons and ascending grades of refinement and joy. No one who shares this vision of human destiny will succumb to narrow theologies or exclusivist worldviews. Let us be secular Hallvards.

"At the very least let us bear in mind the immortal words of the Swedish Lutheran theologian Maldenius: 'In essentials, unity; in non-essentials, liberty; in all things, charity. Thank you.'"

Silas stopped, and the audience stood up and applauded. No shouting or whooping was heard, as at a concert. No one heard Queen Lisbet tell her husband, "My goodness, he gave us a sermon!" or King Gustav's answer, "Yes, but a good one." A solid mass of appreciative clapping went on unabated for two and a half minutes. Silas stood and received it, bowing every half minute or so, looking a little embarrassed.

When it stopped, Ms. Christensen approached the podium as Silas took his seat. "Thank you, Mr. Wyatt. Now we shall hear from Saira Wyatt."

As Saira approached the podium, did she notice the murmur of anticipation in the audience?

"Ladies and Gentlemen, like my husband, I am all too humbly aware of the honor bestowed on me. My gratitude knows no bounds.

"I hope no one minds my using this opportunity for a heart-to-heart, no-holds-barred discussion of Islam's strengths and weaknesses. Muslims make up 28 percent of the world's population, the same as Christians. In the first half of my speech I'll spell out some of Islam's weaknesses and where it needs to change; in the second half, we'll look at its strengths and what keeps me in its fold.

"It grieves me to say this, but Islam is the world's biggest nuisance. Worse than that, where there is a terrorist attack, 95 percent of the time it comes from a Muslim. They are the world's biggest murderers, and their victims are overwhelmingly other Muslims. Why is this? We all know the reason. A minority of Muslims, and I speak now of the Caliphate and their sympathizers all over the world, believe that it is God's will that the religion of Islam cover the globe and weed out all contenders. They further believe that they are required to use any means to achieve their objective, including violence. They claim that Islam is a religion of peace, but their actions make it appear to be a religion of conquest. They cite a few passages in the Quran to bolster their misguided enthusiasm and ignore contradictory passages. My fellow Muslims, do not delude yourselves. The Quran was not a finished document when Muhammad died. It did not exist in book form, and the process by which it was later brought together in the form we know it today was imperfect. Critics have pointed out inconsistencies. To take one example, although it is supposed to be a collection of recitations from God to us, in some passages God is addressed. And there are many other reasons to doubt that the entire Quran was revealed directly by God, and that it is a perfect record of God's revelation to humankind.

"You might assume that Islam would fall apart as a religion if God's revelation were imperfect or flawed. This does not follow at all. Even if the Quran faithfully reported Allah's message to his Prophet, it was a message for a particular people at a particular time in human history. Those people were mostly Bedouins living in a harsh desert region. Their customs were not ours, and the revelation they needed to hear is not in all ways the one we need today. So we must use our intelligence and common sense to cull what is essential in the revelation from what is unessential. Consider, for example, the much-discussed verse 4:34: 'Men

have authority over women because God has made the one superior to the other, and because they spend their wealth to main-
tain them. Good women are obedient. They guard their unseen
parts because God has guarded them. As for those from whom
you fear disobedience, admonish them and send them to beds
apart and beat them. Then if they obey you, take no further action against them. Surely God is high, supreme.' We can question whether God ever said these words to Muhammad, but if
God did, they would not be appropriate for us today. There are
other places in the Quran that strike us today as morally inferior
advice as well, and others that contradict what we know from
science. The lesson to be learned from this is that, while it is
good for the Muslim to seek advice from the Quran—and most
of it applies to all times and places—it is helpful to remember
that if God were to give humanity a new revelation fit for the
twenty-second century, it would differ from the Quran in some
ways. We must not attach ourselves too closely to what doesn't
speak to our better angels.

"Let me reveal a little about myself. My parents were Pakistani, and they insisted that I memorize the entire Quran in Arabic, a language I did not understand; I managed about half of
it by the time I graduated from high school in Brooklyn. I was
never encouraged to read any other book except my textbooks.
As for studying other religions, this was not only a waste of time
but a rebellious act, a sin. In every way it was discouraged. I now
regard this attitude as a pathology. Where did it come from? As
a child I had the fear of hell drummed into me. The thought of
the angels of death interrogating me in my tomb a day or two
after my death struck terror in me from an early age and immo-
bilized my natural curiosity about the world. Only Islam was
worth knowing about. Only the Quran was worth reading. Only
the hadith could be trusted to give me the rules for life. So I, like
so many other daughters of Islam, grew up deferring to men in
all areas of life. I allowed myself without protest to be married

off to a wealthy man as his second wife—that was my fate—
and to be excluded from prayer in the mosque for fear of being
a temptation to men. 'It is for your own safety and comfort,' I
was told. What must Allah be thinking when he witnesses this
self-delusion?

"In some Muslim countries apostasy is considered a capital
offense. Apostasy is leaving the faith, and it is said to disrupt
the peace and harmony of the Muslim community. If the malefactor protests that he is freely following his conscience, that is
no excuse. In several Arab countries non-Muslims are forbidden
to assemble in a church or temple to practice their faith. These
restrictions have no place in America or any other democratic
country, where individual liberties and rights are protected, including the Muslim's. If Muslims are ever to earn the respect
and trust of non-Muslims, they must reject these arrogant, un-
neighborly attitudes."

Saira went on to discuss other "deficiencies," as she called
them. She singled out Islam's resistance to admitting wrong-
doing in its bloody conquests of non-Muslim countries, especially India. "Christians openly admit they committed atrocities
against the Jews, against Muslims, and against each other in the
many wars between Catholics and Protestants," she said. "Why
can't we acknowledge our own atrocities? Not to do so is a sign
of weakness, not strength." And she mentioned Islam's threat to
the world through overpopulation. "The Caliphate's strategy is
to take the world by numbers if not by violence. Do not be deceived. Take your birth control pills."

After further exploring the psychology of Muslims who defend their religion at any cost, she lashed out at it for its treatment of women.

"...There is so much to say on this subject that I hardly know
where to begin. First, a girl growing up in some Arab countries is
lucky if she escapes genital mutilation, while in others the practice of honor killing is still practiced under the protection of the

local sharia. Closer to home, in nearly all mosques women cannot enter the main hall and worship; they must stay behind curtains or be sequestered in dingy rooms. As a result, few women go to mosque except at Eid. Praying as a community and deriving the spiritual benefit of a weekly sermon are reserved for men. Many women over the years have tried to remedy this unfair treatment. A hundred years ago women-only mosques began to crop up in the United States and Western Europe. Women imams called the faithful to prayer, preached the sermon, and worshipped along-side Christian sympathizers and others of no faith. Some were even gay-friendly and challenged the near-universal interpretation of homosexuality as a sin. In Brooklyn where I grew up, two such mosques flourished until they were fire-bombed. In the last century the mothership of such mosques, the Women's Mosque of America headquartered in Los Angeles, gained the moral and financial support of prominent Muslim men. The organization became a force to be reckoned with until their president was beheaded in 2041 during the First Persecution. Since then, the Caliphate has pretty much had its way with these mosques — you all know what happened to the Khadijah Mosque in Manhattan. But since my husband's kids campaign, that is changing, and the Caliphate is on the run. It is of the utmost importance that Muslim women all across the world take this opportunity to open mosques and claim their God-given equality. Eventually, let us hope, Muslim men and women will be worshipping side by side with their families, as do Christians. At the very least, let us adopt the custom of dividing the sexes by only a center aisle, as do our Sikh brothers and sisters."

Saira next asked for Muslim males to reconsider their attitudes toward music. While praising their stand against popular Western music that degraded women and "growled with the stink of hell," she called their ban on sacred music un-Quranic and a "puritanical perversion."

"...Many imams say it's forbidden to watch a woman sing,

even worse to watch a man and woman sing together. Of course, many in America ignore their advice. My question is, 'What's wrong with sacred music *in the mosque*?' I have attended church services with my husband and heard music that lifted me to heaven. Allah loves beauty, and music of the right kind can inspire and uplift. Our great philosopher and mystic Al-Ghazali said, 'Whoever says that all music is prohibited, let him also claim that the songs of birds are prohibited.' Sacred music belongs in the mosque."

She then closed in on her main theme, and it showed in her demeanor. Those up close could detect a fleeting ferocity in her expression.

"The greatest failure of our religion is the belief that it is the only true religion, the only religion that pleases God. It fails to acknowledge the fact that God loves all his creatures equally. It fails to see that God loves the Shia or Yazidi or Druse or Sufi as much as the Sunni. It fails to recognize that God loves your enemy as much as he loves you. It fails to see that he loves the Christian or Jew or Hindu or Buddhist as much as he loves you. It fails to see that men and women for many centuries have been molded into saints by their non-Muslim faiths. It cannot imagine how paradise could be filled with people other than Muslims. It refuses to acknowledge that it is *one* of the paths to God, not the only one. It refuses to acknowledge that humanity's scriptures, including the Quran, are guidebooks, some more inspired than others, but none perfect. It refuses to understand that all of us are the products of the cultures we were born into. It fails to see that men and women are rewarded or punished for their actions, not their beliefs. Can you imagine God sending to hell a twelve-year-old Hindu boy whose life is ended by a twenty-year-old suicide bomber, while rewarding the jihadi with paradise because he is a Muslim? Does anyone really think this? And if he does, how can he love a God so irrational, so unjust, so ignorant of the very nature of his own creatures? And how can he look forward to spending eternity with a God who is such a monster? Let me tell you a secret: the Caliphate is composed of men and women just like him."

Saira paused. She scanned the audience, looked left and right, then up as if in a moment of prayer. She smiled and almost seemed to chuckle as she looked back down at her papers.

"I shall now address the non-Muslim and try to convey the beauties of the religion and why I've stuck with it, in spite of steady exposure to the religion of my husband. First, let me say that the Islam I love is content to take its place alongside, and not above, the other world religions. Well do I know that I would have been a devotee of the Goddess Durga if born in Kolkata to Hindu parents. If I ever forget that, somebody shoot me, please. With that said, I see Islam's greatest strength in its simple, no-fooling-around view of God. In Christianity I often encounter a rich-uncle conception of God rather than a Father to be appropriately feared—a God who dotes on us so much that even if we don't make much of an effort in life to be our best selves, he doles out all the rewards of heaven at the moment of death anyway. Protestant Christians believe even that the sinner's faith in Jesus, faith alone, saves them from hell, and that their deeds are irrelevant to salvation. Islam holds that this attitude discourages top performance and encourages spiritual laziness. Allah is to be loved, of course, but also to be feared—feared not because his judgment is frivolous or arbitrary, but because he expects so much of us. I need him to expect much of me; if he didn't, I would become careless or apathetic. I need to fear his disapproval if I don't do my best. I need him to push me. Eliminating fear from our lives because it is supposedly a bad emotion is unwise and unrealistic. Muslims are not tempted to regard fear in this way. I do not mean that fear should predominate in our lives, only that it is an essential attribute of the human experience. I thank God for his tough love and celebrate the religion that promotes it.

"One of the most obvious ways of responding to Allah with love and holy fear is to pray. Islam not only encourages us to pray, but requires us to pray more frequently than any other religion and in a more kinetic way. From the time I was a tiny girl my mother showed me how to wash up before prayer and how to bow as I prayed. Today I am comfortable praying in any position, but it feels best when I bow deeply and touch the floor. Islam means *submission*, and this posture cultivates a spirit of submission. When a Muslim bows, ideally she is not petitioning Allah for something she wants or doing penance for some misdeed; she is simply recognizing his perfection and greatness, next to which we are feeble creatures. Allah doesn't derive any benefit from our prayers, but we do. Prayer is the cornerstone of our religion. More than a ritual, it is an active conversation with our creator in which we express our wholehearted gratitude for the precious life he has given us. When we pray in this way, the day goes well."

Saira launched into a brief summary of Islam's other Pillars, then brought up Sufism, the mystical wing of Islam.

"...Most of the world, and perhaps most of you, think of Islam as synonymous with the predominant Sunni sect. But it is so much more. Consider Sufism. Sufism emphasizes the power of a sacred word, repeated over and over, to carry one to mystical union with God, whom Sufis call the Beloved. The idea is that the Beloved is always present in the silent depths of the soul, and we can meet him and merge with him as the words of the prayer deepen. Rumi, the great Persian poet, was a Sufi, and he describes his relation with the Beloved as "intimate beyond belief." The journey *to* God gradually deepens into a journey *in* God. Sufis are sometimes condemned by other Muslims for their presumptuous claims of intimacy, but the Quran supports them with the words, 'Wheresoever you turn, there is the face of God.' I am no Sufi and no mystic because I am too worldly. I must be content to enjoy the intimacy of my brothers and sisters I meet at the mosque on feast days. But my admiration for my Sufi brothers and sisters, who live a spiritual life an octave higher than my own, is boundless. And any Muslim who persecutes them is persecuting souls deeply loved by our common Creator.

"Islam is at heart a very simple religion. All that is required is submission to Allah and an acknowledgement of his Prophet. There are many rules, it is true, but most of them are credited to Muhammad in writings that are fallible. If Muslims delight in obeying them—such as eating with the right hand only or turning one's toes in the direction of the prayer—that is all to the good. After all, Islam works for some Muslims because it spells out many of the rules of right living so clearly. The semi-literate mother living in the Sudan or Mali isn't going to bother learning how to think critically, as we are constantly encouraged to do in the West. She doesn't need to. She need only be wisely led. Her deep faith in God and the world to come will lighten her burden: the usual needs of security, comfort, and a place in society that arouse our anxiety and envy will not concern her much. She will live and die swaddled in the certainties of her faith. But some of her certainties are nonessential, and they are certainly not my way. They are not the way of most educated Muslims in the West today, but who is to say that our complex and confusing way of life would be well suited to hers?

"Islam, finally, has given the world splendid architecture, calligraphy, and decorative art. Is there a more beautiful building anywhere in the world than the Blue Mosque in Mazari Sharif, Afghanistan? The arabesque decorations on the walls of our mosques, as at the Alhambra, are almost as spectacular. And the painting and calligraphy in illuminated manuscripts are easily as advanced as anything we have in the West. Even the Muslim's handmade prayer rugs are coveted by the world's art museums. In a word, Islam has much to be proud of in its various artistic expressions.

"There are other reasons I cling to my childhood faith, but

these will have to do. I have surveyed a few of its strengths to show why it deserves your support and even admiration—but most of all to distinguish it from the caricature of it that parades by the name of the Caliphate. Please, I beg of you, keep them separate in your mind. True Muslims need your approval and your love. They represent no threat to the world. They have no more interest in world conquest than the Christian or Jew or Hindu or Buddhist or Sikh.

"I leave you with this thought by Al-Ghazali: 'Declare your jihad on thirteen enemies you cannot see—Egoism, Arrogance, Conceit, Selfishness, Greed, Lust, Intolerance, Anger, Lying, Cheating, Gossiping and Slandering. If you can master and destroy them, then you will be ready to fight the enemy you can see.'

"Thank you."

The audience rose and applauded vigorously, with even a few bravos heard. Saira called her husband to join her, and together they lifted hands held high as the applause increased. The king and queen with their son and daughter-in-law approached them and shook their hands. The committee members followed with handshakes. Then all returned to their seats to listen to Norway's leading soprano, Signe Amdahl, sing the last of Richard Strauss's *Four Last Songs,* with its words, "The great peace here is wide and still and rich with glowing sunsets." Following this, the Royal Family exited the building as all stood and trumpets played. Then Saira and Silas followed to more applause, and it was over.

The captain of their SAS flight home announced to the passengers that they had special guests on board. "Saira and Silas Wyatt, winners of this year's Nobel Peace Prize." Applause and a few oohs and aahs rippled through both cabins.

Halfway across the Atlantic after a short nap, Silas opened up his laptop to see what the world had to say about their speeches. "Generally good," he said. "The best of all is the Council on American Islamic Relations. They say we 'put the Caliphate on notice.' They've truly become our friend. But—well, what could you expect?—another flurry of death threats. And they seem to be, I'm afraid, pointed more at you than me. Outrage over your liberal interpretation of the Quran...and your endorsement of mixed Friday prayer at the mosque."

"It doesn't mean much. We've lived with this all our lives," she said sleepily.

"Well, darling, if you survive this, you'll live to be a hundred and put me in the ground."

A long silence prevailed, and Silas listened to the steady hum of the plane and wished he didn't have to go to work the next day.

Saira said, "Too bad Ethan didn't live to see this day. He would have been so proud of you."

"Of both of us. Look, here's a message from Toshihiro Shima. He must be...he's ninety-six. He sends his *love*—wow, that's something I never thought I'd hear from him. 'As one Nobelist to another'—that's how he signs off...Saira, I am utterly humbled by this whole experience." In fact, Silas choked with emotion as he thought of his meeting so long ago with the great man.

More silence settled in. Then Saira said, "Dear husband, you will find in your desk drawer, next to your will, an envelope to be opened only on the occasion of my death. It is not a will. It is a message to you. It is sealed, and not to be opened on any account until...if I die before you, as I suspect I will."

Silas looked over at her and said soberly, "I certainly hope that doesn't happen."

"I hope it doesn't either." They both sat quietly again. "But if it does, Izzy would be okay. She's twenty-five, and Basil is sure to propose soon."

"What about Eliot?"

"Eliot wouldn't miss me at all."

"Of course he would! Why do you say that?"

"He'd have a direct line to me."

"What do you mean?"

"My silly Silas, how can you forget? You must be tired."

"Oh, that, of course. Our dear, strange son, the clairvoyant. And the spy!"

"Yes, the spy. Funny thinking back to that day at Gracie."

"Well, it brings me right up to the present," said Silas. "How do you like our new home? Seriously?"

"More than I ever thought possible. It's great having a garden I can call my own. Living at Gracie was like living out of a hotel."

They talked on and on about little things, right down to Saira's favorite teakettle with the long, thin, curving spout.

# Chapter 32

Since Saira's address in Oslo, women in Europe and North America rallied to her cause. A succession of women-only mosques opened almost overnight—too many for the Caliphate to keep track of, let alone bomb. Bombings were way down anyway, and support for the Caliphate's dream of world conquest had fallen to 6 percent in the latest Pew poll. The pollsters surmised that approval ratings fell every time one of the old guard died. Clearly the next generation of Muslims was fleeing the dream.

But a few mosques looked forward to a future even more progressive. The Women's Mosque of America, with help from a well-heeled movie producer, was able to buy a vast new headquarters in historic downtown Los Angeles. The producer made four stipulations: that the mosque would change its name, that men and women would share leadership of the mosque on a fifty-fifty basis, that men and women imams would deliver the Friday sermon on a rotating and equal basis, and that men and women and their families would be able to worship together if they chose. Mosques all over the United States, and then Canada and Europe, took note. This was a bold experiment designed to turn women-only mosques into "family mosques." The new thinking was that if you were not a family mosque, you weren't truly progressive. And if you weren't progressive, you were a friend of the Caliphate. The Caliphate retreated more and more underground, but they were far from finished.

The LA mosque was originally a Congregational Church built in 1932, and had long been a popular venue for weddings and concerts. It survived the great quake of 2049 with only minor damage, and its new Muslim owners had big plans for it stretching across at least another century. They could imagine a no more appropriate way to officially open business than to have Saira give the inaugural sermon, or khutbah, in the storied old building. Saira, now sixty-two, was delighted, and accepted.

On an overcast Friday in June, Saira mounted the pulpit with her hair flowing over her shoulders—a symbol not of rebellion but of women's freedom. She told the overflow audience of both genders and all ages that exactly 1500 years ago, in 629, Muhammad was giving khutbahs in the world's first mosque, an open-air building that he helped construct. She gave a history of the Women's Mosque, told how it almost closed its doors after their leader's assassination, praised its present leaders for their courage, and blessed the donor for the millions he gave to buy the church and convert it into a mosque. She made a brief reference to Silas, her "dear husband and partner," who sat unnoticed on the crimson carpet among the crowd.

As she spoke, outside the building two men seated in a car talked quietly and earnestly. The older man reminded the younger, dressed in a coat and tie, that his wife and sons would be well cared for. "Keep reminding yourself what your sons have to gain: a fully paid education in one of Islam's best universities in the Middle East. And your family—sons, daughters, wife, in-laws—you saw the house we'll buy for them. Keep that in mind if you waver. But above all, remember your gift to the world, to Islam, and to our Prophet, praised be his name. And now let me have your wallet and phone, and anything else that might identify you."

The prayers followed, and Saira found her way from the pulpit to the place reserved for her in the front row. The head imam, a woman with a Ph.D. who taught religious studies at USC, intoned the prayer and regulated the bowing. In the back, Silas bowed to the floor and praised his God—the God who lived in the souls of free creatures wherever they might be found across the universe.

Refreshments and lively, excited conversation followed the service. Silas joined Saira and talked to a bearded little man with mirthful eyes who turned out to be the rabbi of a synagogue in

Pasadena. "Well, here we are," he said, "a Jew, a Christian, and a Muslim, with HaShem, the Father, and Allah all squeezed into one Being. It's a day to be remembered, don't you think?" He smiled joyfully, and Silas felt an instant affection for him.

In the car, parked just beyond the entrance to the mosque, the older man said, "When she comes out the door, walk toward her, but not too fast. Make it appear you've come to congratulate her. She'll walk down the steps, probably slowly—I count nine. Try to get to her as she reaches the bottom. Beyond that we can't be sure which way she'll turn. Don't hesitate, not for an instant."

An entourage of female admirers flanked Saira on both sides as she slowly made her way out of the massive double-doored building. Silas walked behind her deeply involved in conversation with his new friend. The sun had broken through the overcast. The lunch crowd had returned to their offices, and traffic along Sixth Street was light. Sparrows overhead twittered gayly. Three or four photographers took pictures of the great lady. A half dozen reporters stood by, waiting respectfully for her to finish her descent. As she reached the bottom stair, a young man pushed his way through the gathering little crowd. He stood directly in front of her and bowed slightly.

Silas heard three rapid cracks, then shrieks. He looked up just in time to see a man raise a pistol to his head and fire. Then he saw Saira wilt on the concrete sidewalk. She looked as if she had fainted, and he rushed up to her, pushing the women aside. "Darling, what...?" Then he saw blood spurting out of her chest through her dress. "Saira, Saira!" He held her head up and tried to hear anything she might say through the screams and yelling. He thought he heard her say his name, then something about a letter. Then very clearly, as her eyes gazed up at the blue sky, "Oh God."

# Chapter 33

On the plane back home the next day, Silas tried to imagine what life without Saira would be like. One of the flight attendants knew who he was, and he melted when he saw tears gathering in her eyes as she briefly pressed his hand. He quietly wept off and on during the long flight home.

When he wasn't thinking of her and speechlessly talking to her, he diverted himself by looking at email and news reports. His children, whom he called within ten minutes of the shooting, told him they would meet him at the airport. Layla, who had recently been appointed president of her university, wrote that she was devastated but would "not be standing idly by." A few of his old colleagues at the *New York Times* sent their condolences. Members of his staff at City Hall, and even two servants at Gracie Mansion, sent their sympathy. Newspapers all over the world lavishly praised Saira. The *Los Angeles Times* headlined its article "Saira Wyatt, World's Best Friend, Assassinated," and showed three photos: Saira smiling as she exited the mosque, her body laid out on the sidewalk in front of the mosque, and receiving the Nobel Medal in Oslo two and a half years earlier. The *London Times* reported that a large gathering of Muslims, many weeping openly, were gathering at Piccadilly Square to grieve the loss of their spiritual leader. *The Hindu* called her "the Muslim Gandhi" and noted that the killer fired three bullets into her chest, just as Gandhi's killer had done to him, and that she died saying the same words Gandhi said.

He read, then quietly resumed his conversation with her, then read some more.

Izzy and Eliot met him at JFK, and together they held each other while Izzy choked with grief. A photographer got too close, and Silas snapped at him. They traveled home to Silas's house in Larchmont north of the City. This lovely old two-story

Colonial home surrounded by lawn and trees, the place that he and Saira had so lovingly chosen, felt to Silas like a mausoleum when he entered. It was filled with Saira's things, but not Saira. A neighbor brought in food, and the little threesome reminisced, not about the great soul the world admired, but the wife and mother they would never see again. Then they retired to their respective bedrooms and tried to sleep. The next morning was Sunday, and Silas suggested they go to church. Izzy was marrying a Muslim, but she could swing either way. To her it didn't matter. God was God, no matter what you called him. Eliot was pliable too, so they went to mass and, as a family united in faith, sent their prayers heavenward. Silas asked heaven to comfort her, then directed his prayers to her. "We miss you, darling," he prayed. "May you be happy wherever you are." But no words came close to expressing what he really felt.

When the kids left the next day, he went for the drawer where her letter was waiting. He had been tempted to open it earlier, especially in their...in *his* bedroom the night before. But he told himself it was better to wait until he was completely alone. He had a hunch Saira had written something remarkable, and possibly upsetting. Before opening it, he leafed through a picture album that Saira had somehow found the time to keep up over the years. He put it down, took a deep breath, and slit open the envelope.

My dearest husband, Silas,
I hoped you would never have to read this. But if you did, I hoped it would follow a natural death, though if I had seen such a death coming, I would have destroyed the letter. The letter you have in your hands assumes a violent death, more particularly a death at the hands of the Caliphate. It is an updated version of the first one I wrote.

Dearest friend and colleague, you and I always knew the risk, always knew what we were in for. There will be grief, but there must be no regrets. My concern is that there needs to be a leader to replace me. Please work hard to identify and encourage her. We have made tremendous progress together, and you cannot afford to let up now that I am gone.

As for you, please push for a Department of Religion at the UN, and offer your services as its head. We have often discussed this. But you never got around to it even though you had the contacts. Please get around to it now. You were once New York's "kid's mayor." It's time for you to become the "kid's commissioner," with the whole world in your care.

I don't know how old our children will be when you read this, but make time for them and for any grandchildren that have come along. You have always had a way of letting me do too much of the parenting. Now you must do it alone—and do it well. It will require sacrifice. I will be watching you from my perch!

But, honestly, I don't think you are capable of such sacrifice. It isn't in your nature, regardless of your love for them. I do not reproach you. But there is a solution. I ask you seriously to consider marrying Layla at some point. She would make a wonderful stepmother for them, and she would keep you on track with your fatherly duties. There is another reason. She would make a good partner for you in your golden years. I worry about what would become of you with me gone. You rarely if ever make friends among other men who are your peers. And that is because you have so few: they are either much older than you, like Ethan and Mr. Shima, or a member of your staff. In all the years you worked at the *Times*, where you might have found peers, we never had anyone over for dinner. I've never seen you with a buddy; you never got around to playing golf. But with a woman—with me, I mean—you absolutely shine. I hate the thought of you being lonely, dearest. Finally, Layla was once my dearest friend. I have never known her equal since. And I am certain she is all too well acquainted with loneliness. It would give me pleasure to see you together and her happy. This might surprise you, for I know you've detected more than a whiff of jealousy in me over her. Believe me, I am trying very hard to overcome it as I write! And I do overcome it. But if things don't work out with her, get a dog.

Finally, if the world to come is as your researches show it to be—and I hope it is, oh, how I hope it is!—I will prepare for us a replica of the house we have grown to love, complete with the garden behind the kitchen window that we have cultivated. I'll be the sweet-smelling yellow rose, and you the high-reaching sunflower.

With all my love, Saira.

"Get a dog." He choked with grief and hilarity at the same time. It reminded him of the Indian jungle when she said, "Get a stick." That was his Saira. One minute the theorist, the dreamer, the aspiring saint, the next minute as down to earth as a groundhog. He ached with love for her as he stared at the bedside photo of her looking out over the water at sunset on Ethan's deck.

Within a week of Saira's assassination, Layla released an official notice on university stationery. Inspired by Saira's heroism, she courted a similar death sentence by arguing that anything short of full equality between the sexes in a mosque was un-Islamic and "repugnant to Allah." Her message, which was meant for American Muslims, went viral around the world. Almost overnight moderate Muslim men awoke to the absurdity of depriving their women equal access to worship in a mosque. Mosques around the country courageously followed the LA example, openly daring the Caliphate to intervene. The Caliphate itself felt so threatened that it actually endorsed the new movement "as an experiment" and wrote off the assassination as an unauthorized attack by a lone wolf. If there was ever an indication that the

Caliphate's ascendancy was ended, this was it. The new question became how the new equality was to show itself. Most called for division of the sexes by a center aisle. Their reasoning held that a man's bowing within inches of a woman's bottom was unseemly and potentially tempting. Others stood for open seating, with no restrictions. A few questioned the need of a full bow, thereby removing the issue of women's bottoms. Mosques without restrictions came to be known as "Family Plus" mosques, those with restrictions "Family Minus." There were many disagreements as individual mosques tried to decide on policy, but no one resorted to violence.

# Chapter 34

Eliot had a slow start finding his way to a career. He wavered between thoughts of being a credentialed Spiritualist teacher, a professor of religion like his father, and a member of the CIA. He knew the world wouldn't survive without the constant policing of the bad by the good; and that recognition, especially after his mother's death, had drawn him to the CIA. He was now in training but had reached a crisis. So he took the train up to Larchmont to talk it over with his father and stepmother. It was a chilly October day, "sweater weather," his mother would have said. He looked forward to the customary walk around the lake that reached almost to the property line out back—the circuit where problems got solved.

He was of average height and by nature slight of build, but he was powerful in a lean sort of way and could bench press 180 pounds. He disliked working out but kept up his DC gym membership and put it to good use. He was accepted by his fellow trainees but, like his father, tended to keep to himself. He told no one about his clairvoyance. He seldom brought it up even with his father—though once he admitted "visiting with" his mother.

Eliot was twenty-five, his father seventy, and Layla sixty-eight. Unlike Saira, who had always worked hard to disguise her age, Layla let it show. Her straight hair down to the shoulders was white and not touched up in any way. Silas concluded she was as free of vanity as she was of jealousy. Saira had been right: He suffered from loneliness, and not even a dog could help much. He married Layla four years after Saira's death with the blessing of both children. Izzy and Eliot learned to love their stepmother and value her advice.

Silas, Layla, and Eliot climbed over the low stone wall and onto the path that circled the lake. Silas lifted the dachshund, Clio, over the fence, and the four set out.

Eliot launched straight into his topic. "Dad, I'm sure you remember what I planned on doing when I was seven years old. Since Mom's death, I've seen myself, almost compulsively, tracking down the Caliphate's hitmen. I've just been consumed with hatred for what they did to Mom. I don't know. Maybe it was just the bar scene the other night with my fellow trainees. I realized we had nothing in common. It became clear my hatred was eating away at my soul. It was slowly destroying me."

They walked along quietly, their shoes crunching on the pebbly path the only sound, as Eliot's latest dilemma sank in. "Well, Dad, what do you think I should do?"

"I really don't know. I thought you were set."

Layla walked just behind the men with Clio as a goose began honking on the lake. She said, "You might consider working for your father at the UN. He could post you anywhere in the world you wanted to go. In that way you'd be fighting the evil of ignorance in the kids of the world rather than crime."

"Working for Dad? Not a chance, that's just too easy. I need to go my own way."

"Eliot, I think that's your ego talking."

"What do you mean?"

"The good you would do is all you should be looking at. And that has nothing to do with who gives you the job. If anything, you'd do a better job because you better understand what's involved. It would almost be in your DNA. You could put into play policies your Dad never dreamed of."

They reached the halfway mark, and Eliot suddenly changed the subject. "Dad, why did you marry Mom instead of Layla. I know how close you were before you met Mom."

"Now that's a question!" said the startled Layla.

"I don't remember," said Silas, looking back at Layla with a grin and a wink. "Do you?"

"Of course I do. It was because you wouldn't convert, you silly man!"

"That's always been the story," said Eliot. "So it's really true you were in love with each other, but religion kept you apart?"

"That's right," she said.

"But you're married now. Why's that? Dad still hasn't converted. Does he now have more mojo or something?" Eliot looked at his gray-haired dad and laughed.

At that instant Clio spotted a rabbit and took off running, the same rabbit he'd tried to catch a million times before while walking around the same lake.

"Huh!" said Silas, "it's just that most people don't have the courage to change, while others do. Same dog, same rabbit, same chase. Most people are like Clio. They never change. Or maybe they just enjoy the chase too much. Layla broke free."

"I was like that rabbit when you first came calling," Layla said. Then she turned to Eliot. "But your dad wasn't like Clio. If he had been, he might have caught me." She looked up at her husband with a teasing smile.

"In which case," said Eliot, "you'd have been my mother. Not a bad deal." He bent over and kissed her on the cheek as they walked on.

"I loved your father more than I let on, even to myself," she said, now all seriousness. "Until I finally told him in that famous letter I'm sure you know about."

That evening Eliot asked his father if he could go to work for him.

Later the same night Silas and Layla lay in their separate beds side by side. Silas said, "Tonight I saw another reason Saira wanted me to marry you. What you did for Eliot will have her rejoicing in heaven."

"You know, it's strange. But when you chose her over me, I didn't feel jealousy. Just loss. Deep loss. I think that's because I saw what a great person she was. Losing out to her was no insult to me."

"Darling Layla, you didn't lose out. My choice wasn't based

on love. I adored you both, but for totally different reasons. There was no way to compare you. A hundred times I tried to figure out who I loved more. It left me in utter confusion. I was exhausted, almost out of my mind. The only thing I knew for sure was I didn't deserve either one of you! It ended by being a choice between living with another man's daughter and my own. Didn't I say that in my letter?"

"My dear husband, it doesn't matter now. All that matters is that I finally caught you. And with Saira's permission."

"And encouragement!"

Layla turned on her side, faced him, and said with a hint of mirth, "Then all that remains to be seen is which one of us you'll choose after we're dead."

He jumped out of his bed, shoved back her covers, wriggled in next to her, and said, "My white-haired jezebel. That you should entertain such a thought. When did you become so bewitching?"

# Chapter 35

Layla, Izzy, and Eliot took turns watching over Silas as he lay dying. Eliot was on watch in the bedroom—it was 4:40 in the morning—but Layla and Izzy remained awake talking in the kitchen.

Izzy just shook her head. "He wouldn't even consider chemo. And now no morphine."

"He's dying just like people 500 years ago," Layla said. "The natural way he called it. It was the same with his colonoscopies. He refused anesthesia."

"What a strange man, my dad."

"So many sides, Izzy. Childlike, vulnerable, sweet. Unstoppable, driven, visionary. Comforted by his deep faith and tortured by doubt. In love with God, but never knowing who God was. Haunted by the immensity of the universe and his own smallness. So many sides. So many sides."

Eliot Stuck his head in the door and whispered, "I think it's beginning."

They entered and saw Silas lying on his back under a thin white blanket. The way his lips moved indicated he was saying something.

"Shhh," said Izzy. They became still and heard something like a feeble whine, a faint singsong whine with a few syllables. They tried to make it out. Izzy bent down close to his face.

"It's a song he sang to me when I couldn't sleep, when I was afraid, when I was a little girl. It's about how God made all things bright and beautiful. It's a Christian hymn."

They listened to the faint words and puzzled over what they could mean. "Dad, we're here," said Eliot, bending down close. Then, as he straightened up, his face took on an expression of surprise and joy, and he said, "Mom's here."

Suddenly Silas sat up in bed, his face wondrously alert as

he stared intently into empty space with arms outstretched and whispered, "Oh, the light. So beautiful. So beautiful." Then he fell back on his pillow with an ecstatic stare frozen on his face.

Within two hours the Albert Einstein College of Medicine picked up his body to use as a cadaver, as Silas had specified in his will. Later in the day hospice came over, disconnected the machinery, and took it away.

"The great man has died," said Eliot, sitting on a sofa between Izzy and Layla as they watched the hospice van drive away.

For a while they sat mutely, each of them exhausted.

"You really did see Mom?" Izzy said.

"Just her face."

"Was she wearing a veil?"

"No."

There was more quiet. Then Layla said, "Izzy, I think it was out of love for you he didn't take the morphine."

"What do you mean?"

"He wanted to show you what dying, dying clean, was like. He wanted you to know you could bring your problems to him any time. He loved you beyond imagining, Honey. You have no idea."

Izzy began to weep, and Layla rose from her seat and wrapped her frail, wrinkled arms around her stepdaughter.

That afternoon Layla and Izzy rummaged through Silas's clothes upstairs trying to decide what to do with them. With his old navy blue suit, the one he wore in Oslo, hanging over her arm, Izzy wondered if he looked down on the earth with something like satisfaction. "The Caliphate's all but dead in America," she said. "His dream has been fulfilled. How many of us can say that about our lives?"

Layla, spreading out his pants and shirts on the bed, stopped what she was doing. She looked out of the window at the great old oak tree in the back yard. Its age must have been three times Silas's, but how gloriously green it shone in its new spring finery. She had been bending over but now stood up. She looked at Izzy and said, "But not everywhere. There's more work to do. There always will be."

"I know, but for now one must imagine Dad happy. Don't you think?"

Then Layla, Muslim to the last, spoke in her quiet and wise way, "One must imagine God happy too."

Outside, on a cool day in May 2150, the earth circled its sun as always, and other suns throughout the universe revolved around their galactic centers as if nothing had happened. But it had. Great numbers of men and women on a small, not especially distinguished planet had learned not to kill on behalf of their sacred certainties.

Roundfire

# FICTION

Put simply, we publish great stories. Whether it's literary or popular, a gentle tale or a pulsating thriller, the connecting theme in all Roundfire fiction titles is that once you pick them up you won't want to put them down.
If you have enjoyed this book, why not tell other readers by posting a review on your preferred book site.

Recent bestsellers from Roundfire are:

## The Bookseller's Sonnets
Andi Rosenthal

*The Bookseller's Sonnets* intertwines three love stories with a tale of religious identity and mystery spanning five hundred years and three countries.
Paperback: 978-1-84694-342-3 ebook: 978-184694-626-4

## Birds of the Nile
An Egyptian Adventure
N.E. David

Ex-diplomat Michael Blake wanted a quiet birding trip up the Nile – he wasn't expecting a revolution.
Paperback: 978-1-78279-158-4 ebook: 978-1-78279-157-7

## Blood Profit$
The Lithium Conspiracy
J. Victor Tomaszek, James N. Patrick, Sr.

The blood of the many for the profits of the few... *Blood Profit$* will take you into the cigar-smoke-filled room where American policy and laws are really made.
Paperback: 978-1-78279-483-7 ebook: 978-1-78279-277-2

## The Burden
A Family Saga
N.E. David

Frank will do anything to keep his mother and father apart. But he's carrying baggage – and it might just weigh him down ...
Paperback: 978-1-78279-936-8 ebook: 978-1-78279-937-5

## The Cause
Roderick Vincent

The second American Revolution will be a fire lit from an internal
spark.
Paperback: 978-1-78279-763-0 ebook: 978-1-78279-762-3

## Don't Drink and Fly
The Story of Bernice O'Hanlon: Part One
Cathie Devitt

Bernice is a witch living in Glasgow. She loses her way in her life
and wanders off the beaten track looking for the garden of enlight-
enment.
Paperback: 978-1-78279-016-7 ebook: 978-1-78279-015-0

## Gag
Melissa Unger

One rainy afternoon in a Brooklyn diner, Peter Howland punctures
an egg with his fork. Repulsed, Peter pushes the plate away and
never eats again.
Paperback: 978-1-78279-564-3 ebook: 978-1-78279-563-6

## The Master Yeshua
The Undiscovered Gospel of Joseph
Joyce Luck

Jesus is not who you think he is. The year is 75 CE. Joseph ben Jude
is frail and ailing, but he has a prophecy to fulfil ...
Paperback: 978-1-78279-974-0 ebook: 978-1-78279-975-7

## On the Far Side, There's a Boy
Paula Coston

Martine Haslett, a thirty-something 1980s woman, plays hard on the fringes of the London drag club scene until one night which prompts her to sign up to a charity. She writes to a young Sri Lankan boy, with consequences far and long.
Paperback: 978-1-78279-574-2 ebook: 978-1-78279-573-5

## Tuareg
Alberto Vazquez-Figueroa

With over 5 million copies sold worldwide, *Tuareg* is a classic adventure story from best-selling author Alberto Vazquez-Figueroa, about honour, revenge and a clash of cultures.
Paperback: 978-1-84694-192-4

Readers of ebooks can buy or view any of these bestsellers by clicking on the live link in the title. Most titles are published in paperback and as an ebook. Paperbacks are available in traditional bookshops. Both print and ebook formats are available online.

Find more titles and sign up to our readers' newsletter at
http://www.johnhuntpublishing.com/fiction

Follow us on Facebook at https://www.facebook.com/JHPfiction
and Twitter at https://twitter.com/JHPFiction